Maladjusted

One Child's Search for Love

by

Jean Taylor

First published in
Great Britain in May 2023

Formatted by Timepiece Press
Loughborough, UK
www.timepiecepress.org

Chapter 1

I looked at my face in the small mirror on the bathroom shelf. Who was that person standing beside me? I moved aside to get myself in the mirror's frame but there was nobody else. That person looking out of the mirror was me, but I didn't recognise myself. My heart began to beat harder and faster and my breathing was too fast. I was dying, having a heart attack. Steel mesh was circling in my brain and I was cold, falling, fading from consciousness, everything dark grey. When I opened my eyes I was on the bathroom floor, face down, dribble leaking out of my mouth and no recollection of why I was there.

I made an appointment to see my G.P and the next morning sat in the chair by her desk and told her what had happened, as far as I could remember. She said I seemed anxious, was there anything wrong? At this point I broke down and wept. My whole life was wrong, everything I did went wrong, I made wrong decisions, got involved with the wrong people, took the wrong turn on the wrong road. I was going nowhere and I wanted it all to stop. I wanted to be somebody else.

Doctor Harty gently probed into the

symptoms and manifestations my mind was punishing me with, diagnosed the bathroom event as a panic attack, talked about some previous experiences, gleaned from my notes, and said that she felt that I needed to speak to a counsellor, to get some help in dealing with past situations that were obviously unresolved.

I protested that I was 51 years old, had had counselling on 3 occasions in the past, none had worked. She knew of a man who she felt certain would be able to help and would request a consultation with me. I would be under no obligation to proceed, but it might be worth a try.

"Hello Julie, can I call you Julie? My name is Matthew. Come in, make yourself comfortable."

I sat in the chair and we looked at each other. After 5 minutes I began to wonder what was happening. Was I supposed to speak first? What was this, some kind of out-staring match?

I started to stand up, planning to leave, feeling intimidated but this seemed to galvanise him into action.

"Why do you think you are here, Julie?"

"Because my GP referred me for counselling"

"It may not be what you expect Julie, but you are free at any time to call a halt ..."

"Okay Matthew. I didn't like the silent

treatment. What was that all about?"

"I like to see how you deal with the silence, it tells me a lot about your mood, state of mind and the appropriateness of counselling. Also, it gives me a clue on how to begin."

"Okay"

"What's your earliest memory Julie?"

"I remember lying in my cot having woken up to find faces looking down at me. It didn't feel comfortable, so I let out a whimper, and they all scampered away and I suppose I went back to sleep."

"Tell me about your house, your family."

"There was *she* my father and me, and we lived in a small terraced house in the outskirts of the city. The whole street was demolished in the late 50's to build blocks of flats."

"Hang on, Julie, who is *she*? Your mother?"

"*She* gave birth to me but was never a mother in any sense of the word. I will refer to her as *she* or *her*."

"Oh, I see … carry on about your house then."

"Our house, number 6, Cowley Street, Old Basford, was the third house up on the right, with an alley between the first and second houses. On the corner, number 2 was a shop, a general grocery shop, and its back yard faced up the street and was bigger than the other houses."

"When you turned left up the alley, our house was the second one on the left with fences on 3 sides, blue brick paving and an outside toilet at the bottom of the yard facing the house."

"I was very scared of the toilet because it was very dark, all the rubbish that blew round the yard blew under the space below the door and it was home to horrible beasts and smells, some imagined and some very real. There was no light in there, and the chain which you pulled to flush the toilet would spin and tap the wall on windy days."

"The house itself was sparsely furnished, 2 rooms downstairs, 2 upstairs, with a cellar and an attic. The downstairs room at the front was unfurnished and rarely if ever used, and anyone who came to the house went to the back door and came into the living room. There was a gas stove in one corner, a table and 2 chairs under the back window and a fireplace, and the stairs went up from the right hand side to the 2 bedrooms."

"My cot was on the back wall of the bedroom overlooking the backyard and the front bedroom was where my parents slept. The attic was Dad's 'den' and full of strange and interesting tools, wood, screws and nails, lots of half-finished bits and bobs, lots of little boxes and packets. Also memorabilia from his days in the RAF."

"Although it was out of bounds to me, I sneaked up there once and found some chocolate wrapped in red and gold shiny paper. Naturally, I ate it and got a good beating. Two good beatings in fact. She gave me a beating because I denied doing it and was shown in a mirror the evidence around my mouth, and later Dad was instructed to give me a beating for being in his den without permission and for finding and eating what had been put there for Christmas."

"The cellar was accessed from the living room and at the top of the stairs was a kind of scullery with a big Belfast sink. The cellar didn't scare me because there was a grille which let in the light, the coal deliveries and the sounds of people passing by, chattering to each other and their neighbours. I knew every inch of that cellar as I spent a lot of time in it. I was naughty and a nuisance and needed to think about improving my behaviour and the cellar was a good place to think."

"Why were you naughty Julie? What did you do that was naughty?"

"I told lies, meddled with things that were none of my business and I wouldn't eat my dinner because Mrs Jones at number 5 gave me sweets and chocolate. And once Mrs Jones bought me an ice cream when the ice cream van had stopped outside. I was playing with the tar running down the road that day as it was very hot and I found some lolly sticks and made tar lollies. Quite a lot of the tar ended up on my shoes and socks and dress, so you can see that I was a naughty child."

"Were you a fussy eater Julie?"

"I didn't like what *she* cooked, it was greasy and had onions and cabbage in it. If I didn't eat it at teatime, I got it for breakfast, dinner and tea until it was gone, or I got a good hiding and was sent to bed or the cellar. We didn't have a fridge until the mid-sixties, and one day I noticed the onions walking on the plate and discovered maggots under the onions. I ran to the sink and retched, and was spared having to sit and look at the plate of yuk for what seemed like hours."

"There was a shop in Lincoln Street that had racks with big boxes outside with dog biscuits in them and I would steal some if nobody was looking, tuck them up my sleeve and eat them when I got hungry. In the other direction on the same street was a greengrocer who had lots of fruit outside too and I would stroll past with my hand out, grab a plum and run."

"One day he came running out of his shop and chased me, shouting that I was a thieving little bugger and if he caught me, God help me. I wet my pants in fright, but I could run a lot faster than him. However, he found out where I lived somehow and came to our house and told my parents to stop me stealing his fruit."

"When I went to my grandma's and to school I would eat everything on offer. Grandpa used to say, 'fill your boots, Julie. I reckon you've got hollow legs!' The school dinners were so good I would hang around after school and forage in the dustbins for something to take the place of the nasty things waiting at home. Then I would go to the park across from the school to eat my 'treat' and hang around till I thought my dad might be home from work."

"Why didn't you go straight home?"

"If my dad was there *she'd* have to have a good reason to wallop me, and Dad used to stick up for me if he could. He would pay for it later. I would lie in bed listening to her shouting at him - probably pushing and poking him as I'd seen her do when I was spying on them - and calling him weak and spineless. Sometimes I heard *her* slap his face and I would think that it should be me, not him."

"When he was told to show me who was the boss, he would take off his belt and head upstairs. We had an unspoken agreement. He would belt the bottom of the bed, then I would scream and yell and cry. Then Dad would say 'who's the boss?' I would whisper '*She* is,' and then, making sure *she* heard, 'you are, Daddy.'"

"'Be a good girl then, Jules,' he would say, wiping his eyes. I always wondered why he let *her* do those things, until I was grown up enough to know that when you love someone, you can put up with a lot more than you should."

Chapter 2

"You've said you spent a lot of time hiding in the park and wandering the streets, Julie. Weren't you frightened to be out on your own?"

"Not really. There were always other children playing out, older kids. So I felt safe and didn't think anything awful would happen to me."

"Across the road at number 9 lived an old lady on her own. My dad said her name was Mrs Parker. If she saw me playing in the street on my own, she would often bring me a sweet or a biscuit. Each time she would say, 'what's your name, young lady?' I told her it was Julie but she must have forgotten as she asked the same question every time she saw me. Once I made up a name, Deborah, but she gave me a sharp look and a frown and said she thought my name was Julie. One day I decided it was my turn to ask a question."

"'Can I call you Anosey?' Looking surprised she asked why I would want to call her Anosey. 'My Mum says you're Anosey Parker,' I replied innocently – I had no idea that it wasn't a name."

"Another time she asked me to go to the Post Office to post a letter and buy a stamp for the next letter. When I came back, I asked Mrs Parker why the lady behind the counter said,

'Yes, me duck?' when it was my turn to be served. With a sly grin Mrs Parker suggested that next time she called me a duck I should say 'quack quack' to see if she laughed. She didn't. She chased me out of the Post Office, threatening to box my ears if she caught me. I preferred my ears on my face and not in a box, so I avoided the Post Office for a while, and hoped that word wouldn't get back home and cause trouble."

"There were a few times when I knew I'd be in real trouble when I did get home, though, like when me and some school pals dared each other to climb a tree with a long thick branch overhanging the lake in Vernon Park. I was last, and just as I got to the end where everyone was clinging on for dear life and the branch was inches from the water, it snapped and we all got soaked. A couple of hours later I ran indoors, straight upstairs, changed my clothes and stuffed the wet ones under the bed. Of course, they were found a few days later. Another spanking."

"Then there was an older boy who the other children said was a dumbo and only played with little children, but he followed me when we went searching for branches to make a den and when nobody could see us, he asked me to pull down my pants. I asked why, and he said he just wanted to see. I pulled down my pants and he just stared, but it felt a bit creepy, so I pulled them up and ran. I didn't see him again, thank goodness."

"Another time I walked back through the park and out the bottom gate, crossed Vernon Road, over the railway crossing, climbed over the wall into Billy Bacon's field, where I played a lot. The River Leen ran through it, shallow at the end by the railway station and deep where the railway crossing crossed the main road."

"There were often gypsies camped there and I was told not to go near them, but as I was a naughty child, I disobeyed. I got on well with the gypsies, they showed me nothing but kindness. I enjoyed reading their comics - the Beano, the Dandy and, best of all, Bunty - or drawing in the caravan if it was wet or cold. On warm days I'd be paddling in the river and fishing with the gypsy children. A peripatetic teacher would come to teach the children to read, write and do sums; they either thought I was one of the gypsies or were just pleased to have a child interested in learning. No doubt that was how I was able to read before I went to school."

"The gypsy kids had fishing nets and jars and laughed a lot. We played daft games and sang silly songs, and I'd often go home with nettle stings, filthy and with my legs stuck with leeches from the river. Dad would drop a little boiling water from an eye dropper on their heads and they would curl up and fall off my leg. If I tried to pull them off, the heads would stay in and get infected."

"One day, I couldn't see the children playing, there was no campfire and the caravans looked locked and deserted. Just the horses and one dog tied up on a long rope that I hadn't seen before. My heart started to beat fast, I was a bit afraid of big dogs, and I wasn't sure if the rope was long enough for the dog to reach me before I could get to the part where the river was shallow."

"It was barking furiously, leaping and straining on its string, and then the worst thing happened - it broke free and I had to get in the river as far from the bank as possible and wait. That was the only time I was really scared. The dog bit my arm just as I was wading out to the middle of the river. I was terrified and started screaming. The lady from the Post Office heard the noise and came out to see what it was all about. She shouted that she was going to telephone the police. The police came and caught the dog, got me out of the river and took me home. They advised that I should have an injection in case the dog had rabies and said that the dog would be put down, which I didn't understand then meant it would die. One injection and a good hiding later I decided I had better steer clear of Billy Bacon's field for a while."

"The other time I was frightened was when I used to walk back home from Kathleen's house. Again, it was as late in the afternoon as possible. *She'd* got a cleaning job - which makes me smile as our house was never clean — but she arranged for me to be looked after while she worked. There was a bakery and shop on the corner of Lincoln Street and David's Lane, by the railway crossing. The couple who owned and ran the bakery had a daughter, Kathleen. *She* would take me to the shop and Kath and I would spend lovely long afternoons drawing and colouring and making up stories in the big room above the shop window. Kath was very sweet-natured, and she always let me choose first, even though she was older than me, and she had what seemed like hundreds of coloured pencils and a stack of colouring books. One or other of her parents would check on us regularly and bring lemonade and sometimes a cake or bun each."

"I loved those happy times, but I dreaded the walk back. The public house on that side of the road had beer delivered in wooden barrels on a cart pulled by two dray horses, big stocky animals with nasty tempers. I was used to the gypsy horses in Billy Bacon's field - they were smaller and more interested in munching grass than in keeping an eye out to kick you. I used to talk to them, and sometimes got a grunt in reply. But the dray horses were a different kettle of fish. There was no talking to *them*. Their tails would flick, they shook their manes, and hooves would fly at you with deadly speed and accuracy. I'd keep close to the wall and try not to look at them, but at the same time try to be aware of any small movement that indicated they were getting tetchy. Usually I just crossed the road to avoid them."

"I asked at home if I could have some crayons and a colouring book and was told that only children who had rich parents had such luxuries. So I decided that I was going to be rich one day, and in the meantime I'd pray that *she* kept her job and I could keep on going to play with Kath."

Chapter 3

"Did you pray a lot ,Julie?"

"We went to church on Sundays. The church we went to was on Queensberry Street, opposite my nursery and school and I believe it's still there and in use. I never spent more than a few minutes at a time in church, before joining the line of children filing into the room next door, where a nice lady taught us songs and read us stories. We always said prayers. I prayed mostly that we'd have enough money to have nice things. I thought life would be better if we had enough money."

"There was one bad thing that happened at church. One time we went to church and this time there were a lot of people there. I sat on the seat at the front swinging my legs and looking at the pretty patterns on the ceiling, and humming to myself, a tuneless collection of notes that wandered into my mind, while the ladies chatted and gathered round us and Dad sat on the end of the seat looking uncomfortable. Throughout the next 10 minutes there was singing and incomprehensible muttering which I didn't understand, but knowing that I must be quiet I started counting the coloured squares in the window, by colours, starting with the yellows, of which there were fewest and ending with the reds which were most numerous. In this state of reverie I was suddenly jolted to attention by the calling of my name, and quickly snatched up by my dad followed by *her*, and we all processed to where the man wearing a black dress was standing waiting."

"From my father's arms I watched, mesmerised as the floor before us opened up, making me feel dizzy and revealing a large square of water, bluer than the sky, pure and clean. Before I had time to consider what might be about to happen, I was passed to the man in the black dress, and before I had time to wriggle out of his grasp or shout for help, he was walking down the steps and into the water. I froze, rigid with fear. Were they going to drown me? Surely not, not with everyone watching! Is this my punishment for being a naughty child?"

"Then, as the panic turned to the need to scream, my head was under the water, my body, rigid and kicking followed and the scream was swallowed by the blue water."

"After what seemed like an age and the urge to breathe in air took over, arms flailing to get me out of the water, I was raised out of the water and set down by the edge. Shaking and sobbing, I hardly noticed the towel being wrapped around me, and I was suddenly in my father's comforting arms again."

"It was some time later when I was able to speak about it that I learned that this was my baptism, aged 3 years and 5 months. And I was never again able to look at deep water without my heart rate quickening."

"After that I always asked the question, 'are we going in church today?' My dad would answer, 'I'm going to church, you're going to Sunday school and your mother is going to cook Sunday lunch.' Sometimes it would be, 'after church we're going to Grandma's and your mother is going to have a rest.' 'Yippee, Grandma's, Grandma's, Grandma's!' I would reply. *She* would glare at me and her eyes would go to the wooden spoon in the utensils jar by the stove."

"At Sunday school we learned about God and Jesus and angels and prayers. I would pray that *she* would start to like me, and stop shouting at my dad, and that I could go and live with my grandma. But because I was a naughty girl I wasn't surprised when the prayers didn't get answered. I prayed a bit less often, and then only when I'd done something I shouldn't have done."

"Did you ever go out as a family, Julie?"

"Yes, I have 3 very clear memories. Once we went to the cinema and got fish and chips on the way home: It was 1956 and the film was called 'Private's Progress' and very funny, although I didn't understand much of the army scenario. But Ian Carmichael in the leading role got drunk and said his name and rank were '999 Picklepuss', which I found very amusing for a long time."

"Another time was when we all went to the fair on Billy Bacon's field and I won a goldfish for getting a ball inside a jar. I put the goldfish in the river, as I thought it would be lonely in our house in a jam jar."

"Then there was the time we went on holiday. I don't know where we went, but I remember Dad walking us round the town, going in the arcades where he would put a penny in a machine and sometimes it would push more pennies off a shelf and we all got another go with the prize pennies. We ate ice creams but were sworn to secrecy and told not to tell our mother. Dad laughed a lot, and I enjoyed having just him and my brother for company, but he kept looking at his watch - because, he said, he had to collect *her* from the hairdresser at a certain time. I wondered then what *was* a certain time, as I thought all time was certain."

"*She'd* had her hair permed at the hairdressers. She had a thing about curly hair."

"What do you mean, a thing?"

"Her hair was straight and mousy brown.

Her sister had lovely blonde curly hair which was very much admired by everybody. *She* was jealous and got obsessive about it, I realised when I was older. She spent a lot of time trying to make her hair curl and I remember distinctly being told to go and amuse myself elsewhere for a couple of hours and being glad to escape from the smell of Twink perm lotion, which hung around all day."

"What did your Dad look like ?"

"He was tall with dark hair cut short, and he looked good in a uniform. I knew this later, going through photographs of Dad in his Scouts' uniform and the R.A.F uniform."

"*She* was short and slim, probably attractive ... well, to my dad at least."

"What was it like when all the family was together, at weekends, holidays?"

"Oh yes, there was a fourth memory! It was the Christmas Eve trip. On Christmas Eve we'd get the bus into Nottingham. In Slab Square in the city centre was a crib scene, with painted plaster versions of Joseph, Mary, Jesus, the shepherds, Wise men and various animals, in various states of shabbiness. You could walk among them and stroke the animals, so the sheep were repainted more often as a result."

"You could toss a bit of straw about when the parents' eyes wandered to the tea stall next door. Health and safety regulations hadn't been invented then, so it wasn't unusual to see children running round at high speed, occasionally leaping onto a horse or cow, or swinging from the scaffolding poles that held the 'stable' together."

"Other stalls would be selling fruit and veg. Geese and turkeys freshly killed would hang from butcher's hooks. Turkish delight and crystallised fruit would tempt us in exotic eastern-decorated bamboo boxes and the stalls themselves would be gloriously decked out with real greenery, firs, holly, ivy and mistletoe. Oranges were wrapped individually in coloured tissue, ready to go into the children's Christmas stockings. Christmas trees could be bought there for 5 shillings, rooted for replanting, or to be chopped up if you only had a small backyard like us."

"Then, back home on the trolleybus and *she* began peeling the potatoes and carrots, putting the cross on the base of each Brussels sprout so you could boil them to death. Then stuffing to make, mincemeat - which had been made in October along with the Christmas cake - would be spooned into the pastry cases made earlier and then put into the oven to cook. No cellophane, plastic or cardboard to bin, no preservatives or fridges to make things last."

"While the food was prepared in the kitchen, Dad would be in the front room, which was only used for big events, keeping me and my brother from getting overexcited by decorating the Christmas tree, which he'd put in a big tub, usually a bucket."

"There would be baubles made of glass to hang on its branches, a straw angel on the top, cotton wool snow, fairy lights with tiny coloured bulbs, which often died or tripped the wiring, causing sparks to fly, and figures made from wood, alabaster or paper, from the scene at Bethlehem, baby Jesus in a tiny crib."

"Then, if we had any energy left we would glue strips of coloured paper into chains, which Dad would hang on the walls while we slept, and which would greet us on Christmas morning after we had delved into the Christmas stocking, (one of Dad's socks) and taken out the orange, notebook and pencil, a toy car or small doll and a whistle or other musical item with which to annoy the grownups. My favourite present of all time was a wind-up sparkling Cinderella and Prince Charming musical toy which danced when you wound it up. It came to Granny's house and stayed there! A few years later I discovered that it was Granny, not Father Christmas who provided it."

"You have a lot of memories and you give a lot of attention to detail Julie. There seems to be a fair amount of emotion attached to them?"

"I loved Christmas. Dad was a jolly sort of person in those days, always whistling and singing, his face suited a smile. Even *she* seemed happier, and not so inclined to punish me."

"When Dad got married, he had left the Air Force. His uniform was hung behind a curtain in an alcove in my bedroom and I sometimes looked at it and tried to imagine him up in the sky in an aeroplane. The reality was that he had a great deal of trouble getting a job, and there were often tears and tantrums as yet another job went out the back door and *she* would be 'scratting to make ends meet,' as *she* would say."

"Do you suppose that might have accounted for her lack of jollity?"

"I'm sure she had a hard time of it. Of course, post war rationing only ended in 1954, so a lot of the things we take for granted now were not available during my early childhood. The few toys we had were mostly made from wood; Grandpa and Dad made a wooden horse on wheels and Dad would pull me on it round the small blue brick back yard. I had a whip and top, a hula hoop and a mosaic set of shaped and painted red, blue, yellow and green flat bricks, all handmade. I would wrap the leather thong round the whip, set it on the linoleum covered floor and pull the whip away leaving the top spinning. In theory you could keep whipping it to keep it spinning, but I wasn't so good at it and one day I got mad with it, told it that it was a stupid daft and silly thing and threw it on the coal fire - then cried for an hour because I had one toy less. I had a wooden yoyo, too, which took a while to master, but at least it didn't get condemned to burn to ashes."

"Do you ever think about what it was like for your parents, Julie?"

"From what I know now, after reading the letters she sent to Granny, *she* was much more at home in an office. Domesticity – and, it would appear, raising children alongside running a home on very little income - took her out of her comfort zone. She found it challenging."

"I just wished that it would always be Christmas, with bright lights presents, nice food, everyone smiling and a lot less telling off and smacking!"

Chapter 4

"Would you like to tell me about your Grandma, Julie?"

"I …, she …"

"You don't have to tell me if it makes you upset. Here, have a tissue."

Matthew passed the box of tissues over to me. I took a fistful and sobbed into them for a while, then decided I would play her down so that I wouldn't get upset again. That, however was impossible.

"My Grandma was the rock that kept me safe, Matthew. Everything about her was good, loving, caring. She was always helping people, generous with her time and her love. She was one of God's angels, although she didn't look a bit like the pictures of angels in the prayer books and paintings in the Sunday School room."

"Two years before she died, she was awarded the Freedom of the Borough for her services to the Community. But to me she was everything – parent, friend, confidante, encouraging me and supporting me in all that I did, forgiving what I did wrong, a source of stories and wisdom. Nobody could have loved me more than my Gran. She did discipline me, and I always knew when I'd overstepped the mark. If she told me to behave, I usually did. I asked her one day, after she told me to behave, if I had been have, which tickled her pink, but that didn't stop her from refusing to buy me an ice cream from the van just inside the University Boulevard entrance to Nottingham University, when we went to walk round the lake and look at the Rhododendrons one Sunday. I'd been told not to be cheeky and had pushed my luck after hearing Granny say that Dad looked like a dog that had lost its bone. I was laying the table and said I would put Dad's cutlery on the floor under the table in case he found his bone. I got a clip round the ear from my dad for that!"

"You must miss her, Julie?"

"More than anybody could imagine. Even though it's been 37 years, I still miss her and think about her every day. Of course, *then* I didn't have any idea that I would have to manage without her. She was always a part of my life."

"She and Grandpa would pick me and Dad up from Church and take us back to their house, where we would spend the afternoon and have lunch and tea. Then they dropped us home in their car – it was a Ford Consul, MRR 902 and I can still remember the registration. I learned about what was going on at home by sitting quietly drawing and colouring in at Gran's dining room table, crushing the sugar, or untangling string which Gramps brought home from work and took back - untangled by me - on Monday morning."

"What was crushing the sugar about, Julie?"

"Oh, it used to come in blue paper, it was oblong and as hard as rock. My Gran would get a big sharp knife and cut it into 4 square blocks then give me a rolling pin and I would bash it into granules, taking care not to bash it off the table onto the floor as that would encourage ants and mice. The bungalow was wooden and the spiders were absolutely massive - I often thought they were mice when they scuttled out from behind the furniture. Oh, and the string was fascinating to unravel and I would put the short pieces in my pocket to take home. I would eat it when I was hungry but being indigestible it went through my system and meant spending quite a long time in the loo, as you can imagine."

"While I was busy crushing and untangling, conversations went on in the kitchen which I wasn't supposed to be able to hear, and I began to understand the dynamics of my so-called family."

"*She* didn't like Grandma and thought she interfered too much in our lives. But was it interference or was it really helping? It seems that when Gran was elected to local government, she found out about demolition orders and was able to buy our house for peanuts, as it was due for demolition but still had a 10-year period before that was likely to happen. Gran also knew when house repossessions were going to happen and most of the furniture we had came cheap from such events. In my child's mind I could only think how great it was that we got so much for so little."

"Of course, now I can see that it might be annoying to not choose your own house and furniture. What was worse, though, was that *she* constantly mocked my dad, sniping that he was a mummy's boy and how he was married to *her* but hadn't really left home. There was perhaps some truth in that."

"When my dad was born there were complications which meant that Gran had to have a total hysterectomy. That meant removing both her uterus and ovaries. It was lucky that they'd both survived, but there would be no brothers and sisters for my dad. Granny was one of 12 children born, seven who survived, so I don't know if it was a relief or a source of sadness to have only one child. Anyway, my dad was very fond of his mum and dad, and *she* was jealous."

"My Gran told Dad off too, sometimes. She said I was being neglected, that I was too thin and I always had bruises that you don't get from being clumsy. He should do something about it, she said one Sunday in late June, especially now that I had a brother."

"Wow that must have been a surprise Julie. We'll talk about that next week, okay?"

"Okay Matthew"

Chapter 5

"Hello Julie, how are you today?"

"I'm fine Matthew, how about you?"

"All good. Shall we go back to your brother being born? When did that happen?"

"A month before I was two. I was born in hospital but *she* refused to go to hospital the second time around, so he was born at home. It was horrible, the noise she made, yelling and screaming as if she was being murdered. I escaped down to the corner shop but the children were at school so I had to go down Billy Bacon's field and play with whoever was there."

"My dad came to find me when it was getting dark and told me I had a baby brother and that his name was Michael. I wasn't very excited, but I did think that he might take up a lot of *her* time and keep *her* attention and the wooden spoon away from me a bit."

"I was right about that. *She* would take him shopping in the pram, leaving me locked in my bedroom. I hated not being able to go out and play, but it was one of the punishments for going up into Dad's den. She made him put a bolt on the outside of my bedroom door. I suppose it was warmer than the cellar, and I had a few books and toys - again what my grandparents had provided - that had survived *her* wrath and not been consigned to the dustbin."

"I kept a lot of toys, books, shoes and clothes at Gran's house. I would put on pretty dresses, shoes and hair ribbons as soon as I got there, and make everyone laugh by trying on Gran's shoes and hats in the front bedroom. After playing with the toys and pestering Grandpa to give me a ride on the garden roller or the lawnmower, it all came off and got put away for next time when it was time to go home."

"I never wanted to go and would sometimes cling to Granny and cry, begging her to let me stay and never send me home. But of course, that wasn't going to happen, and I think I knew that even then."

"Funny though, *she* obviously liked this new baby brother, and my life was less scary for quite a while. I did wonder whether my life would've been different if I had been a boy."

"Do you think it would 've been better, Julie?"

"I'm not sure. I think she found him easier than me, he slept a lot and wasn't as lively and curious to know what was going on as I'd been, according to the letters. I found out over the years from Granny that *she* came from a dysfunctional family. Her mother was an alcoholic and her father often 'absent'. Her sister was very pretty and clever and could do no wrong, whilst they used to gang up on her and ridicule her. When she started work, they made her hand over her money and helped themselves to her belongings. It all sounds like Cinderella, doesn't it? And I suppose she saw my dad as the Prince Charming who could take her away from 'all that.' But wouldn't you think that if they made her life so miserable she would make sure that it didn't happen to her daughter?"

"Unfortunately it doesn't always happen like that. Some adults repeat the behaviour they suffered from with their own offspring."

"Yes, I've heard that, and it was a long time before I decided that I dared to have children myself."

"That's something we will address later, Julie. Let's carry on with your childhood for now. You had a lot of freedom when you were very young Julie, how did you spend your time?"

"Mostly in Billy Bacon's field. There were almost always children there and they always let me play with them. We played games like 'king of the castle', where you had to stop the other kids from reaching the top of the hill (either a small mound by the fence, or the pile of coal in the station yard), and if you kept the 'intruders' at bay for a count of five you were king of the castle. 'What's the time, Mr Wolf?' was another game where the elected wolf turned his back on the rest, and would ask the question, 'What's the time, Mr Wolf?' while moving forward. Wolf would say, for instance, 3 o'clock and turn round, and if he saw anyone moving, they were out. When he said, 'dinner time!' he would catch the nearest child and they were out. This could go on for a long time."

"'A leg and a wing to see the king' was a game where two bigger kids picked up a smaller child (often me) by the arms and legs, and the two would swing the victim back and forth 'to see the king' and then count 1-5, and on 5 they would let go. The victim had to hope that (a) they were not close to nettles, (b) they would land on their feet and (c) they didn't rip or break anything."

"On wet days we'd sneak into the waiting room at the station and play 'I spy' and charades or guessing games until the station master found us and sent us packing. On cold days we'd find the houses with chimney walls on the side and huddle backs to the wall in twos or threes, depending on the chimney size, and stamp our feet and rub our hands to keep warm."

"We also played 'chicken', where we knocked on someone's door and if we heard somebody coming to open it, we would run and hide. Sometimes the canny ones would come out of the back door, down the entry and up the road and catch us. That often ended with wet pants! The other version of 'chicken' was dangerous and involved waiting for a bus, lorry or van to approach and at a given signal from the rest, the 'chicken' would either run across the road in front of the vehicle and get a round of applause, or consider it too risky and get a chorus of 'chickin, chickin, gonna get a kicking!' I must've been very close to injury or death more than a few times as I was afraid of very little. I could run fast too!"

"When the gypsies were camped on the field I wasn't supposed to be there, so I pretty much had to hide, either in the caravans or the railway station or in the park. The caravans were very beautiful inside, cleaner than my house by a long chalk, and they had beautiful ornaments which I was allowed to look at and hold. I couldn't understand why people said they were filthy vagabonds and thieves and couldn't be trusted. I never had anything but kindness from them, apart from the dog that bit me."

"When Michael was 2 and I was 4, I started nursery."

"How was that, Julie?"

"It was mostly good. I did try to escape a few times, not because I didn't like it, but because there were things outside and up the road I wanted to explore, and I could see the older children from the attached school going over to the wasteland across the road, next to the church. I found out later when I started school that a witch lived in the tumbledown shed on that wasteland and if she caught you, you would end up in her cauldron as dinner."

"But nursery was good because you got milk to drink, food to eat and people to listen to you. What I didn't like was having to have a 'sleep' after lunch and having to lie down. I had no need to sleep and got into trouble on many occasions for wandering around the building, and was often given a picture book to look at. Once, I swapped the picture book for Janet and John and sat reading out loud. The nursery teacher came and tried to take the book off me and I didn't want to let go. 'I'm reading it!' I scowled, and was marched down the corridor to the boss lady's office, and the nursery teacher told the boss lady what had happened. Boss lady sent the teacher back to the other children and invited me to read to her. Which I did."

"'Who taught you to read?' she asked, smiling. 'The gypsies,' I replied, smiling back. 'Oh, we have a clever one here!' she said in a not very pleasant way. 'Perhaps this clever child should be going to school and not nursery!'"

Chapter 6

"So did you go to school after that?"

"Yes, I did. My journey to school, which I was expected to walk alone, took me from number 6 Cowley Street, Old Basford in Nottingham, about half a mile to Southwark Street Junior school."

"At the corner shop at the bottom of our road I turned left to walk along Lincoln Street, which was cobbled then in the mid-fifties. I passed the butcher's shop. The butcher - appropriately - was called William Bacon, and he owned the field behind his shop which the River Leen ran through, as did the railway line to Basford Station."

"I walked past the Co-op, with its boxes of dog biscuits in boxes stacked on a shelf outside, which I thought was odd because a stray dog could easily steal them if it was big enough. Past the hairdresser, who always seemed to have curlers in her hair. Past the greengrocer with his tempting array of fruit and veg - his plums were almost as sweet as my Gran's."

"Past the pub, the Fox and Crown, which was one of the oldest pubs in the district. The building once housed a debtor's gaol and behind the pub was a bowling green, hence the word 'crown' in the name, and was where crown green bowling was played. The last duel fought in Nottingham took place behind this pub in 1807. My dad told me all this when I was in my teens."

"The Fox and Crown often had the dray cart and horses outside, delivering the barrels of beer, and as I told you, I'd cross the road on those days as the horses were nasty. Where Lincoln Street met David Lane was the bakery where I used to go sometimes to play with Kathleen and her colouring books and pencil crayons. They had to be sharpened a lot, I remember – I loved to watch the fine brown fan-shaped shavings come out, with tiny bits of colour on the end."

"I crossed the road there and went up the steps of the bridge across the railway line to stand on the top as the loco passed underneath, sending up a great puff of steam and smuts of coal and smoke with an interesting smell, and the haunting hoot of the whistle on foggy and wet days. I was afraid of the steps with blank spaces between them, I thought I might fall through and get run over by the train. When I arrived at school I'd be told to go and wash my sooty face, and on bad days it would be scrubbed by a teacher."

"Choices now. I could go over the zebra crossing and straight up Southwark Street or turn right onto Vernon Road then left into Vernon

Park gate. That was my favourite route, but if the train was late I didn't have the option as it took longer. I knew that because the gates would be closed a long time before the train arrived."

"In the park I walked past the pond where me and the other kids had tried to climb along the overhanging branch and all ended up in the water when it snapped. From the pond up the path to the warden's house - quietly, to avoid 'Parkie', as he hated children who made dens, tore branches from trees and filled him with rage. He was often heard shouting 'bugger off yer little bloody vandals!', getting redder in the face and more enraged when we were far enough away to turn and laugh at him, putting our thumbs on our noses and waggling our fingers at him."

"Beyond Parkie's house were the swings and roundabout, which we played on at lunch time and again after school. It was a delight and a nightmare. If big boys were there, they made us sit on the long bench swing sideways. It travelled east to west with a boy operating each end. Their goal was to go fast and high with us sliding both ways until we fell off. The council put square handles over the sides some years later, but I still have a piece of gravel embedded in my knee from when I slammed into the ground."

"Without the big boys, we could swing, slide, dig in the sand pit and make ourselves dizzy on the roundabout to our hearts content. There were two parallel bars of different heights, where we hooked one leg over the top, clasped our hands underneath around the leg and used the other leg to propel us around the bar like spinning Catherine wheels."

"Alternatively, you could sit on the bar and fall backwards using your bent knees to hang on to the bar and swing till you felt the blood rush to your head. It didn't work if you tried falling forwards, you just fell off and broke your specs, if not an arm or leg, or worst scenario, your neck."

"Beyond this was the gate which came out onto the top of Waterford Road, opposite the vicarage, where a plum tree and a pear tree were out of sight of the vicarage window. The Vicar must have wondered why they bore very little fruit!"

"If I turned left at Parkie's house I was out onto Waterford Road opposite the school side entrance."

"The Southwark Street route crossed the River Leen, which was culverted under the road from the weir. Then I crossed the bottom end of Waterford Road. Walking straight up, I passed the sweet shop - slowly, my gaze lingering on the fruit salad and black jack sweets, four for a penny, gob stoppers, sherbet fountains, multicoloured Kayli in a pointy bag with a liquorice dabber to dip in it, multicoloured liquorice laces and Allsorts, Torpedoes - red ones you used as lipstick, elastic bracelet sweets, love hearts, Parma violets and bubble gum. All yummy, but needing money. We were not allowed bubble gum as - we were told - it stuck your insides together and you would have to go to hospital to get them separated. Not worth the risk, I figured."

"Up to Queensberry Street, turn right and I have arrived at school."

"How did you feel about starting school?"

"It was fine. I had something to do all day and enjoyed learning. I was always the youngest in the class though, and, while I could stick up for myself and didn't get bullied, I did get called names. I had a lazy eye and wore glasses from the age of 2 and a half. So it was 'four eyes,' 'bozeye' or 'squinty-face', and they were National Health specs, round, coming in pink, blue or brown plastic frames: mine were brown and often patched up with Sellotape when I broke them."

"*She* had got some dark maroon material that looked a bit like denim but was stiff and scratchy, and made me three identical dresses as school wear. We didn't have to wear school uniform, so the other children thought I only had one dress and called me 'one frock Goldilocks.'"

41

"I loved learning. I can remember very little about the teachers, but there were three teachers I did not like at all. The headmaster who would come round the classes and ask questions like 'which is heavier, a ton of lead or a ton of feathers?' I would put my hand up enthusiastically and answer, 'a ton of lead,' and then become the laughing stock."

"The arithmetic teacher, Mr Holmes was dubbed 'Omo' as he always wore a brilliant white shirt, and Omo was one of the early washing powders. He had braces to hold up his trousers and would stand with his thumbs hooked in the braces while we chanted our times tables. He also had a whip with leather strips and a plaited handle, which lived on a shelf under the blackboard alongside the board rubber. He would stand in front of the class, running the leather strips through his fingers and looking very much as if he would enjoy using it on our backsides. This was the indication that a mental arithmetic test was about to happen, and the classroom was silent apart from the slapping of the whip. The aura of panic and alarm gathered over us. Strangely, I don't recall him ever using that whip."

"The other teacher I didn't like was the art teacher, who would circulate as we drew or painted and would stop at my desk and sniff, then stare at my hair as if she expected things to fly out of it. I think it was because I had taken to going around with a girl who had moved into the area to live with an aunt. She always had wet pants and headlice and was often sick, so there were not many children who wanted to be near her. Peggy was her name and she was as thin as a clothes peg, but she seemed to like me and waited after school for me. We crossed the road to the park and played till dusk."

"You say she seemed to like you. Do you mean she did like you?"

"Maybe she did, maybe she had no other friends, as she was new to the area."

"What did you two talk about?"

"Mostly about things we didn't like."

"What didn't you both like, Julie?"

"Mothers. Hers had sent her to live with her dad's sister, and because the house was small and there were 4 cousins, she had to sleep on the floor of the landing. They used to put paraffin on her head at night and in the morning there were dead lice all over her pillow and it made her stink and be sick. You know about mine,' *She* didn't really want me."

"We didn't like being different. We just wanted to be like other kids, and talked about the things we wanted - nice clothes, birthday parties, things that normal children had, gardens to play in with lots of friends, colouring books and crayons, things we could only dream about, things that the other kids talked about and boasted about."

"Did you dream a lot?"

"Yes I always dreamed, some good dreams, some bad."

"Tell me about them"

"I was never able to look at deep water without fear, and water often appeared in dreams of drowning and woke me up screaming with my heart pounding. The other dreams I had were about running away from something evil that wanted to kill me, often snakes, giant crabs or black spiders."

"Peggy dreamed about beautiful places, tropical islands, sunshine and music, and she told me about the white cat."

"Did you say 'the white cat'?"

"Yes. She would call 'here pussy pussycat,' and a huge white cat came and sat by her side. She could climb on its back and it would take her to all the beautiful places. It could fly too, so she never had to worry about getting away from the bad things."

"I tried to call the white cat when I was going to sleep, but it wouldn't come to me. Instead, I found that I could fly. I had to run quite fast, then jump, at the same time putting my elbows out to the side and pressing down as I left the ground, travelling upwards fast at first then slowing down and becoming horizontal like an aeroplane. I saw so much from this vantage point, a magical world of fantasy and colour. Larger than life and harmoniously interactive, it thrilled me and aroused my curiosity. I was able to drift down at will, pulling in my elbows, to inspect what called to me, and then rise again to sing with angels and rest on fluffy clouds."

"That sounds marvellous, Julie, I think your imagination was perhaps helping you to deal with the bad things?"

"Yes. But then I would wake up and nothing had changed - until I did something really bad. She had stopped telling me I was naughty as it didn't bother me anymore. When she hit me I was determined not to cry or care about it, so she would hit me harder, banish me for longer. And you can make the word BAD sound so much worse than naughty."

Chapter 7

"So what did you do that was bad, Julie?"

"The older children at school had made things in craft lessons and the school was selling them to raise money, maybe for a charity, I don't remember. It was impressed upon us how important it was to buy what the older girls and boys had made and to raise money. So, I looked at all the things again. I'm not sure what else there was, except for a magnificent boat with sails which I could just imagine sailing on the river in Billy Bacon's field. The kids I played with would be able to have a go with it and they would be mightily impressed with me."

"When I got home and Dad was there, I asked if I could have some money to buy the boat. It was one shilling (5 pence in today's money). I was told in no uncertain terms that all Dad's money was needed to buy food and clothes and pay the bills, and the boat was not something we needed."

"Well I thought it was something I needed and what's more I would have."

"So I waited till everyone had gone to bed, and gone to sleep, then I crept downstairs in the dark and felt my way to the back door, where Dad's jacket was hanging, and I knew there would be money in it. However, it was on a coat hanger, on a hook, and the hook was at the top of the door – out of reach! I got a chair from the table as quietly as I could, and it was big and heavy, so not an easy thing to achieve. I stood it by the door and climbed up, but I could only just reach the top inside pocket. The side pockets were empty, so I knew his wallet was in the top pocket. Out came the wallet and in the dark I fiddled around and took out a banknote, having no idea how much it was, and put the wallet and the chair back where they belonged, then crept back upstairs and into bed, stashing the note under my pillow. I was really excited next day and could hardly wait to get to school and buy the boat."

"At playtime I went to the classroom where all the crafted items were, and a teacher that I didn't know wrapped up the boat and asked me for a shilling. I proudly handed over what I now know to be a pound note, twenty times one shilling."

"'Oh dear,' she said, 'that *is* a lot of money. I don't have enough change. Let me think ...'"

"She then summoned the headmaster, who looked at me for a very long time, then asked me where I had got so much money from. I said my dad had given it to me, and the headmaster said that the 19 shillings change was too much for me to carry around at school, and he would give me a letter to take home asking one of my parents to come into school and collect the money from his office. He would keep the boat safe in his office, he said."

"That was a long day. Although I was only six, I realised that there was a lot of money involved. Which meant that it would be missed. Which meant that I was in a lot of trouble."

"I was in a head spin all the rest of the day, and couldn't even eat my dinner at lunchtime. I was praying in my head, 'God, if you are there, please get me out of this mess,' over and over and over again. Just before the end of the last lesson the school secretary cane into the classroom, spoke to the teacher, who pointed to me and she came and put the letter, addressed to Dad, down on my desk."

"Well, that was it. I wasn't going to take that letter home. No way could I come out of this one alive!"

"And then ping - an idea came into my head, and I thought yes, thank you God. Run away, that was what I had to do. I cast around in my head for ideas about where I could go. I thought perhaps the Police Station, they were so nice to me when *she* and I got taken there after shopping trips."

"Then I thought, no. I had done something

which even I had to admit was bad, and wrong. The only person in the whole world I could run to and not get punished for it was my grandma."

"As Dad and I got picked up from Church at the end of Queensberry Street on Sundays, I had memorised the route from Church to Gran's. It was around 5 miles, took 15 minutes by car in those days and (I discovered later), around 2 hours on foot."

"I set off when the school bell announced the end of the school day, feeling a little excited, a little scared, and after an hour of walking, more than a little hungry as I'd had too much on my mind to check the school dustbins."

"The second hour, I began to wonder if anyone had realised I was not on my way home. The gypsy children were absent from Billy Bacon's field, so the only place anyone might look for me was the park, which was very big and didn't close till dusk, which was beginning to close in as I headed up Gran's street. I ran up the drive and stretched up to open the latch on the back door. When I walked in Granny was standing at the sink and she dropped a plate in shock when she saw me."

"'What on earth ...? Why ...? How did you get here?' she asked, and my grandpa came in from the front room saying, 'I thought I was seeing things when you ran up the drive!'"

"He had been closing the curtains when he spotted me. 'What's this all about?' he said sternly.'"

"The letter popped into my head and then out of my pocket and I started to cry. Granny put down her tea towel, kicked the broken plate out of the way, picked me up and sat both of us down in her big armchair, shooing grandpa back into the front room with her free arm. She took the letter out of my hand and put it on the table. 'Now, are you going to tell me what the letter is all about?' I looked at her face through my tears, and it was not a cross face, not an accusing face, but my granny's kind face."

"'Oh, but I can hear your tummy rumbling - you must be hungry after such a long walk.' She had obviously worked out that I had walked to Beeston. 'Talking can wait, would you like some bread and butter and my lovely homemade raspberry jam?'"

"Well of course I did, and she waited patiently till I'd finished. I asked if she was going to read the letter, but she said she wanted to hear what I had to say first. So out it all came, every sorry detail, and I started to cry again. She stopped me by saying that she knew that I knew that what I did was wrong, but it wasn't the end of the world. However ... I had to face up to the fact that it would have to be put right, and the first step was to go home and tell Daddy that I was sorry. She made a quick phone call. They were the first to have a landline in the area and it was a party line with the neighbour. I was too tired to realise that we didn't have a telephone at our house. Then we all got in Grandpa's car and he drove us to my house. When we got there Dad was waiting outside, which I didn't think was odd, as it was dark and he often came out in the dark to smoke a cigarette and look for me. He and Grandma had a conversation on the doorstep, then they both came to the car."

"'Come on then, Jules, let's get this over and done with,' said Dad.

'Can Gran and Gramps come in with me?' I asked, and Gramps sucked in his breath and said that was not possible. I gave them both a big kiss and said goodbye. I didn't know it then, but it was going to be nearly a year before I saw them again."

"Why was that, Julie?"

"Next time, Matthew. I'll tell you next time."

"Okay, Julie."

Chapter 8

"You left me with a cliff-hanger last session, Julie. What happened to make it a year before you saw your grandparents again?"

"Where do I start? To sum it all up, that letter was my ticket out of one life and into another. It seems that teachers at the school were worried that I was being neglected, that the stealing was a sign of behaviour that was causing them concern. *She* had been prosecuted by the police after 3 incidents of shoplifting and was due to go to court. She had also been reported by a neighbour for leaving me locked in my bedroom while she went out shoplifting. The Child Welfare Department had been notified and had contacted the school, and they wanted us all to meet up at the school on a certain date to discuss the situation. On that day I was told that I would be going 'to the countryside' to a convalescent home for children. It was in Woodhouse Eaves in Leicestershire, thirty-odd miles away. A half-hour drive by car, but as we had no car, half-a-day on three different buses."

"How did you feel about that?"

"Quite pleased really. When it was explained that convalescence meant recovering from something bad, I thought that I would finally become a good girl, and then everybody would love me. I was told that I wouldn't see my family for a long time, but that they would be kept informed of my progress, and would be contacted if there were any problems."

"And were there any problems, Julie?"

"Oh yes: you don't become institutionalised overnight. There was a regime which we all had to conform to, discipline was strict, personality was discouraged, learning was put aside - apart, that is, from learning what happened where, how and when. I was punished when I wet the bed. I knew where the downstairs toilet was, but not the upstairs one and there was nobody to ask in the middle of the night. I was made to wear a nappy which everyone could see, and the kids laughed at me and held their noses. I was then given a guided tour of the building and shown where everything would happen. The bedwetting only happened once. I began having strange dreams though, where I was dying in hospital and my relatives came to see me and were crying and being sorry for treating me so badly."

"What did the dreams mean do you suppose, Julie?"

"I don't know Matthew, but maybe it was because some of the children there had been very ill. Maybe some had died, or maybe it was because it had been a Sanatorium where people would certainly have lost their lives. It was a strange place at night, maybe there was an atmosphere that I was sensitive to, who knows?"

"Mmm, interesting. Carry on."

"We all played games after breakfast - outside when the weather permitted. 'The farmer's in his den' was a favourite.' A girl had come into the home a few days previously; she too was six, and we were told her name was Dolly and she had spent her life in a cupboard. We all found her a bit scary."

"We talked about her, tried to imagine how she would look and how she might feel, but the reality when she was brought out to play made us all silent. She was as white as a bedsheet, just skin and bones, could only make noises, didn't speak and they put her in the middle with the leader. We all formed a ring around her and danced in a circle singing,

'The farmer's in his den,
the farmer's in his den;
Ee eye add-i-o,
the farmer's in his den.
The farmer wants a wife,
the farmer wants a wife;
Ee eye add-i-o,
the farmer wants a wife.'"

"A wife was chosen by Dolly pointing at one of us. In this way Dolly had inside the circle a wife, a child and now was looking for a dog."

"Oh no!"

"Absolute dismay, horror even. It was me. I went and stood as far away from the three in the middle as I possibly could, but worse was to come. The last line was 'we all pat the dog' and I was summoned."

"'NOOOOOOOOOOOO, I WON'T DO IT!' I yelled.

'And why won't you play the game, Julie?' I was asked.

'I don't want to be touched by a skellington, that's why,' was my answer. For that I spent the rest of the games period facing the oak tree, which meant that I couldn't see what was happening, but a member of staff was watching me. It was a relief not to be close to Dolly, though."

"Poor Dolly, didn't you see her as someone who had been treated badly, not unlike yourself, Julie?"

"After a while I did feel sorry for her. I think it was the exposure so quickly into our midst that frightened me, and the fact that she didn't look human. As a child that was the reaction that, as an adult, I would be ashamed of, Matthew."

"Tell me more about your days at the convalescent home, then."

"I found out later that it had recently been a

sanatorium for adults with TB - it had areas that definitely resembled a hospital. When I was there it was a convalescent home, but it was much more than that. Generally speaking, it was for children who couldn't function in society as they were, but had medical and physical needs which needed addressing."

"I believed I was there because I was a naughty girl – but I've discovered that I was seen by the people in authority as neglected and my behaviour a result of this neglect."

"We all queued up for everything - wash, teeth cleaning, nit nurse, medication, a teaspoon of malt (yummy) and a teaspoon of cod liver oil (yuk) mid-morning, evening cocoa and our meals. It was hell to me as my life had had no parameters of care, no structure until I started school. I was a free spirit, streetwise, intelligent but emotionally undeveloped, and I found the restriction of my freedom difficult to bear."

"Again - and this was probably so that the staff got time out - if we had behaved well, in the afternoons we all trooped down a tree-lined grassy avenue to a space, a very small field, with our mats and some sweets."

"There, we had to lie on fold-up beds and sleep or at least keep quiet for what seemed like hours, till a bell rang from the house to signal the next event on the agenda."

"I was often without sweets, mostly because I was adjusting badly to my restrictions and sweets were only given for good behaviour, so I didn't get any. The only thing that kept me from completely losing my rag was that one day I spotted a fox, its bright eyes peering through the hedge, checking us out. I kept very still and the fox came through the hedge and trotted down the avenue, turned right at the bottom then disappeared through another hedge."

"I had never seen a fox except in story books and it was a fine specimen, reddish brown with black and caramel markings on its face. I was ecstatic, and every time we went down there in the afternoons I would watch the hedge, desperate to see the fox again. I never did see it again though."

"Did you make friends in the convalescent home, Julie?"

"There were probably about 15 children in the home and I found that most of them were either recovering from an illness, not expected to recover or exhibiting strange behaviour, and in retrospect I'm not sure that it was good for us all to be lumped together under one roof. But we were and we had to get on with it, like it or not. The fact of being there enforced my feeling of being different and not acceptable socially, although at age six to seven I saw it as punishment for all my crimes, and I had an expectation that after a while I would become a good girl and could go back home. I kept waiting and hoping for a sign that I was getting better."

"There was only one child that I could call a friend, his name was Julian and he was permanently in a wheelchair because, he said, he'd had poliomyelitis as a baby. He was ten years old but couldn't read and he asked me one day if I would read to him. We had free but supervised access to a good selection of books. He'd heard me reading out loud to one of the supervisors and said he liked my voice and the way I read, making things seem real and alive. He was not a handsome boy, but he had a mischievous smile and a twinkle in his brown eyes, and I liked him better than any of the other children because he smiled a lot."

"I asked him once why he was always smiling when he seemed to have very little to smile about. He told me that we have 43 muscles in our face; if we frown we use all 43 muscles but it only takes 17 muscles to smile."

"I wondered who had told him that, and what else he knew. So I decided that we were friends, and when I started to read to him, he began to tell me stories from his family life and also gave me sweets which he saved from his daily ration and which I ate in secret. We never disagreed about anything and he was a source of delight to me."

"His was a sad story. His parents - who obviously loved him very much - were killed in a car crash. He had no siblings because, he said, his Mum and Dad wanted to give him all of their time and love. He had one aunt, but she was unable to look after him, as she was blind and deaf. I never will understand what kept him smiling, but he was the first boy I wanted to hug and kiss, something I never dared to do!"

"Was there anything else about the home that made you feel good?"

"I suppose I got used to the rules and regulations, the curriculum and the lack of freedom. I was safe, fed regularly and if I made an effort to do something good, I got praise for it. This was very new for me, and it made a huge impression on me. I guess that was the beginning of learning to please adults to gain self-esteem."

"Was that a good thing, Julie?"

"Ah! The six million dollar question! If I had known then what I know now I would say no. But I had to find out the hard way, didn't I?"

"Did your family visit you in the home?"

"No, but I didn't expect them to. I'd been told that they couldn't come and see me. I was surprised then one day, when, after our evening meal, we were having 'quiet hour' before getting ready for bed and a supervisor came to me and told me to go with her as I had a visitor. I was terrified as I thought it must be somebody who had come to take me away to somewhere worse because I was a bad girl. I had spat out the cod liver oil on the floor that morning, saying that it was disgusting, a word I had picked up from one of the cleaning staff, and I'd guessed its meaning…"

"Imagine my surprise, then, when I went into the office and there was my dad! We ran into each other's arms and then we were both crying, my dad saying, 'oh my little Jules, I've missed you so much!', and me just sobbing and not knowing why."

"He said he felt so alone at home on his own, and just had to break the rules and come and see me. He said how well I looked, no longer the skinny Minnie with matchstick legs, and I had some colour in my cheeks, all of which I had failed to notice, but I was glad he was pleased with me."

"I asked him why he was on his own at home, and he looked at the supervisor, who shook her head slightly then looked at me. I looked from one to the other until my dad said that my mother and Michael had gone away for a while, but they were being looked after and there was nothing to worry about. I gave him a big hug, and before we could go back into the sad place, he held me at arm's length and said,

'Come and see my new motorbike – well, it's second-hand, but new to me. You can come and wave goodbye?'"

"To this day I don't know how he managed to get to see me but after that I got some respect from the other kids and felt a bit special."

"How long were you living in the home?"

"I'm not sure, probably about a year and a half. I found out later that on the opposite side of the road was the Zachery Merton convalescent home which was built in the 1940's to house injured war veterans. The home also contained a mental hospital wing known as Beacon Lodge, which would take adults and children with mental illness and severe physical problems. This was shut down and reopened several times when the N.H.S took control of it but it finally shut down in the 1990's. A builder bought the site, about 20 years later, demolished the hospital/convalescent home and built seven luxury houses.

"The convalescent home was being closed down and some children went back to their homes and families. I was told one day that I was going to live somewhere else, in a children's hostel. I didn't know what a hostel was but the word sounded like 'hostile' and I did know what that meant!"

That was the beginning of a new chapter in my life and I am going to have a lot of difficulty talking about it."

"Okay, Julie. You're looking tired, so let's call it a day. You've done well and dealt with a lot of emotions today. I'll see you next week and we'll talk about the new chapter in your life when - and only when - you're ready."

Chapter 9

"I'm sorry about last week Matthew, I just couldn't face it."

"And how are you feeling today, Julie?"

"I think I'll be okay."

"We won't rush into it, and if at any point you need to stop, that's fine, we'll stop. Do you remember that when you were on Ward 37 you were shown how to deal with panic attacks and stressful situations?"

"Yes, but I don't want to lie on the floor!"

Matthew laughed. "You won't have to lie on the floor, we can stay just as we are. Are you ready?"

"Just give me a minute, Matthew ... Okay I'm ready."

"Okay, take a deep breath in, Julie.

Hold it ... one, two, three, four, five.

Breathe out ... one, two, three, four, five.

Repeat five more times.

Relax your hands.

Now your arms and shoulders. Tighten your hands and arms then relax them.

Screw up your face then relax your face muscles.

Straighten your legs, tense the muscles in your legs and feet, and then relax your feet, then your legs."

"Close your eyes and imagine you are somewhere beautiful, peaceful. It can be a real place that you know, or a place in your mind that you have created. Where is this place, Julie? Describe it to me."

"I'm at the end of a long drive. I'm opening the black wrought iron gate, Now I'm walking towards the bungalow, stopping to look at the flowers. There are antirrhinums, heads like little dragons and when you press the flower head they open their mouths - we called them snapdragons. Marigolds with lovely orange heads and a strong smell. Calendulas - similar but yellow. Violets in between the wallflowers. Bellis Perennis - the botanical name makes an ordinary flower like a daisy sound grand. Osteospernum. Lilies of the Valley. They smell heavenly but spread everywhere if you let them. Periwinkle."

"Then, at the top of the drive I pass the lilacs, with their heady scent, in profusion over the veranda and the front steps. I'm turning left, into the covered-in brick extension. The bungalow is made of wood, stained dark. The extension houses the toilet and the washhouse."

"I go out of the side door, up the garden path, past the enormous pink fuchsia which Granny had grown from a cutting she'd pinched from a stately home she'd visited. Left to the garden roller sitting idle by the rhubarb patch and the raspberry bushes, then on to the vegetable garden, where rows of beetroot, onions, carrots peas and a great wall of runner beans are on the left, gooseberry and redcurrant bushes on the right alongside the potato patch. After the potato patch is the garage, also brick, at the top of the drive. I keep going, down to the two sheds, passing the plum trees - a Victoria plum, a yellow plum and a purple one, turn left past the strawberry raised bed - remind me to tell you about the frogs!"

"Turning left by the strawberries I see the chicken coop, with a fox-proof wire fence and the henhouse, where Granny and I would collect the eggs by lifting the lid to the laying boxes on the outside. On the other side is the orchard, with its apple, pear and cherry trees. I'm turning back down past the lean-to on the side of the bungalow and then into the rose garden which follows the front garden down to the road, via the lawn with another four fruit trees and some holes which Grandpa put in so we could play mini golf. This is my paradise, my go-to place where nothing can get to me. A place where I can wander at will without the black dog following me, growling at me. I am safe here."

"Hold that thought Julie. When you're ready, in your own time, tell me about the hostel."

"Dad and I had to go to Nottingham to see somebody in the Child Welfare Department about moving me to the hostel in New Balderton, just outside Newark. There were two people in an office, an elderly man who said he was a doctor and a youngish woman, whose name was Miss Perkins. They explained what would happen and asked if we agreed to the move. My dad said yes, but he wanted to see the place first and would like me to go with him. There was a whispered conversation between the doctor and his assistant and we were told how to get there on the bus."

"We caught a bus from Woodhouse Eaves two days later, into Loughborough, changed there for a bus to Nottingham, then another bus to New Balderton. Altogether it took about four hours."

"When we got to the hostel we were met at the door by a woman who said we should call her Matron. She was around 45, I think, and seemed friendly. She showed us the dining room, the playroom and the dormitory where I would sleep. The children were all at school, some next door at the secondary school and three at the junior school about half a mile up the road."

"We sat in her office, a large room on the front right-hand corner of the building with a desk at the back and three chairs and a coffee table by the window. My dad asked lots of questions, till I started yawning and then we left and went back on the bus to Woodhouse Eaves. Dad asked if I liked the hostel and I said it would be alright."

"The day came - I was moved in with very little in the way of possessions and told what the daily routine would include. Get up, get dressed, make bed, eat breakfast, go to school, eat lunch at school, come back, play till 5:30, eat the evening meal, 6 o'clock write letters, older children do homework, go to bed, sleep. It didn't seem too bad."

"The reality was defined by the other occupants of the hostel, however, and they were very different from the children at the convalescent home. From them I learned how to shoplift, swear, climb trees and steal fruit, answer back when adults complained about my behaviour, and to fight."

"I had no clothes of my own, so the morning rush to the airing cupboard to get the best knickers - with no holes - and clothes that fitted me was a battle which I rarely won, being one of the smallest and youngest children, and so I wouldn't do handstands at school against the playground wall because I didn't want people laughing and pointing at my holey knickers."

"I can't remember much about the food, but I would sneak downstairs sometimes in the middle of the night and raid the store cupboard, where sacks of dried prunes sat alongside paper sacks of sugar, custard powder, raisins and on good days biscuits."

"I walked the journey to school Monday to Friday with three children who were full of mischief. We would jump over garden walls, steal things, kick anything that was kickable, with one of us (guess who?) acting as lookout. The headmistress had a car and drove past us to and from school. When she called me to the office, I knew why - I had been spotted. So I was punished, usually with a rap over the knuckles with a wooden ruler. I was gullible and generally if anybody got caught doing naughty or silly things it was me."

"There was an old-fashioned wood burner in our classroom which we would cluster around in winter and warm our hands. It had a safety guard to keep us from getting too close, but there were always risk takers. I was dared one day to put my hand on the wood burner, and, never able to resist a dare, I leaned across and put my hand down flat on the top."

"There was an awful smell of burning flesh and tears came to my eyes when I felt and saw the damage. I had Kettering Boiler Co. Ltd in blisters on my palm. Mr Bullock, our teacher, chose that moment to enter the classroom and was very concerned when he saw the blisters. He sent me to the headmistress to get my hand treated (he said) and the treatment it got was to be turned over and the knuckles rapped with the ruler, causing bruises the next day."

"I did get better at avoiding detection over time, but it seemed I was always in trouble at the hostel."

Chapter 10

"I was surprised, in my second week at the hostel, by a call to go to the office, and to find The doctor there. He was, he said, hearing from Matron that I was getting into trouble because of my behaviour. He wasn't pleased with me, and I had to admit that I was doing things which I wasn't proud of myself."

"The doctor sent Matron out of the room to supervise supper. Then he drew the curtains, locked the door and told me to bend over the armchair by the window. My knickers were pulled down and I saw him reach for a cane on the desk. I shut my eyes tight and waited for the beating."

"Three hard smacks across my bottom, and then he said to stand with my feet apart. Then the cane was being pushed between my legs into the place we don't mention, but Grace said was her fanny, and he was chanting,

'In-with-the-good-out-with-the-bad, in-with-the-good-out-with-the-bad, in-with-the-good-out-with-the-bad.'

AND IT HURT."

Chapter 11

I am shaking, sobbing, my face behind my hands registering nothing but the recalled pain. Matthew came over and put his hand on my arm gently, holding out a box of tissues with his free hand.

"Take the tissues, Julie, we'll take a break. Breathe in - count to five. Breathe out. Shall we stop there?"

"Yes, but I don't want to go yet. I feel too broken."

"We'll talk about something else then, Julie. Would you like to tell me about the frogs?"

"Yes, the frogs. When I spent time with my Gran on Sundays ... to tell the truth, I used to follow her round the house and garden like a shadow till she gave me something to do. We would feed the hens, pick fruit, dig up vegetables."

"Sometimes, if the phone rang, she would tell me to go find something useful to do. One day while she was on the phone, I set off down the garden to find something useful to do. My attention was grabbed by a movement in the strawberry bed. On investigation it turned out to be a frog, and as I watched, several more appeared under the leaves. I noticed that some of the fruit had been nibbled and I was cross that the frogs were eating *our* strawberries. After a short search I found an empty watering can and heaved it back to the strawberry bed - with some difficulty, as it was a big copper watering can. I caught the frogs, five in all, and put them in the watering can. Then I heaved the whole lot to the back door just as Granny was coming out."

"What have you been watering?" she asked.

"I told her what I'd done, expecting her to be pleased, but she frowned, looked me in the eye and told me that the frogs were eating the *slugs* which were eating the strawberries, and now the slugs would get to eat *all* the strawberries. I was very sorry and thought she was cross with me. But she looked at me hard for several seconds, then she put her hand over her mouth and laughed and laughed and then some more, and I found myself laughing with her."

"'Oh my life,' she said, 'your face was a picture of tragedy!'"

"She had to explain what tragedy was, then, and then she suggested we put the frogs back. Three of them had jumped out of the watering can, so I was kept busy catching them, then we put them back in the strawberry bed."

"That's a lovely tale, Julie. Your Gran was a very special lady, wasn't she?"

"Oh yes, Matthew, she was an angel."

"Can we go back just briefly to what

happened in that room? I know it was awful, and you did well to get it out in the open, Julie. How long did this go on for?"

"It continued for most of the time I was there, roughly every two or three weeks."

"Did you not tell anyone Julie?"

"I was too ashamed of myself to tell anyone, and afraid that everybody would believe I deserved it, or that it would lead to more, worse things, more awful punishments. I did try very hard to be good, but if I hadn't done anything bad he would just say that I needed to be reminded what happened to bad girls and would do the same thing again."

"One day, Matron told us at breakfast that the doctor would be coming for tea later. I was in a right state, shaking and feeling sick. I couldn't finish my breakfast and I went to school by myself, trying to hatch a plan to avoid seeing the doctor."

"I was in luck as the last lesson of the day was needlework and the sewing room was at the school annexe about two-minutes' walk away on the other side of the road. I decided that I would find somewhere to hide and not go back to the hostel. Again, my luck was in. We were making skirts, dirndl skirts with a ruched elastic waist and a wide hem. The teacher said that if anyone wanted to stay after school to finish their skirts she would be there until 5 o'clock. When the parents came to collect the girls, they either took them home with their sewing, or agreed to come back for them at five."

"I was so pleased to be able to stay in the warm and made sure that I didn't finish the hemming until the teacher said she was locking up and going home. It was growing dark, but I took my time getting back to the hostel, and was surprised when I got back to see there was a police car outside."

"I strolled in, clutching my skirt, looking for Matron to show it to her. She came out of her office looking worried, a policeman stood holding his helmet just behind her. When she saw me, she looked relieved at first and then very angry, asking me where on earth I had been till now. Did I know that the police were out looking for me and they thought somebody had taken me? I thought to myself that would have been fantastic, but I said I was sorry - I was just finishing my sewing at school."

"I asked if the doctor was in the office and was told he had left 15 minutes ago - yessss! - but she said he was displeased with me and would be coming later in the week to deal with me."

"I started pulling bits of my hair out, making my head bloody and sore and then scabby. I would pick the scabs off, and then that made my head look messy. This kept me busy until the time I dreaded was getting closer. I knew exactly how he would 'deal with me'."

There was a pause. Matthew sat up straight in his chair and I could tell he was uncomfortable with what I might say.

"Did he deal with you, Julie?"

"Well, this is weird, but I started praying really hard to God that I would never have to see him again. I didn't hold out much hope, but it was about two months, I think, before I *did* see him. I came back on my own from school one day - the other three were doing some shoplifting in the sweet shop. When I got to the dorm to take off my blazer and school uniform, I noticed that there was a door open at the end of the corridor, which I had never seen inside. Being curious, I went to investigate and there was a lady sitting on the bed with an open suitcase at her feet. She sensed me staring, turned and looked at me, unsmiling."

"I'd half turned to get back to the dorm and avoid a telling off when she said, 'come on in, then, and tell me who you are.' I hesitated, thinking it might be a trap, but when she said, 'and then I'll tell you who I am!' I grinned and she grinned back."

"I went inside and looked around. She patted the bed beside her and said, 'go on, then, you first.' I sat beside her on the bed and told her about me - not much to tell - and my dad, my brother. She said, 'don't you have a mum, then?' I must have waited too long to answer, as she said, 'okay, we'll come back to that.' And then she said her name was Jane Collins - I should probably call her Miss Collins, unless we were completely alone. She was, she said, here to do some training as part of a course in Psycho-something. I asked her how long she'd be there and she said six months, which sounded, to nine-year-old me, not far short of a lifetime."

"I also asked her what she would be doing with us and she said it would have to be arranged, but she would tell us all as soon as she knew."

"I was a bit cheeky, and I asked her how old she was. Twenty-two was the answer. 'That's too old to be my friend, isn't it?' I whispered. She looked me in the eye, waiting till I stopped looking away and fidgeting.

'Nobody is too old or too young to be somebody's friend,' she said. 'But friendship has to be deserved. If you treat me with respect, I will do the same to you. If you behave badly, I can't be your friend - unless you are sorry and you change your behaviour.'"

"I wasn't too sure what respect was, and when I seemed a little perplexed, she said respect was having regard for the feelings, wishes and rights of other people, or not forcing your own opinions and wishes on them. This gave me a lot to think about."

"Miss Collins was introduced to us all at teatime and from that day until the day I left she was someone I would ask many questions, save many thoughts to tell her and generally be grateful that she was there. She looked at my scabby head and got some cream or gel to put on it."

"Jane also told me that every time I wanted to pull my hair out I should come and find her. When I did just that, she took me up to her room, sat me in the chair, then sat on the bed and read or told me stories. She told me to take a strand of hair and make a kiss curl with it, then she fixed it into place with hairgrips. When the story was finished, she took the hairgrips out and I left with a big curl in my tap-water-straight mousy hair and a smile on my face, which she showed me in her dressing table mirror. I have to admit that I pretended to want to pull my hair out a few times just to get the story and some attention, and she had to stop 'encouraging me' to spend time alone with her. She said I could suck the end of a strand of hair when I felt sad or angry, and I did this until my mid-teens."

"Jane asked if she could take any child that

was interested in going to church into Newark on Sundays. A bus ride! Newark was an interesting town and we visited many of its churches. Jane said she was not 'religious' but she tried to be a Christian, and we had some very interesting experiences and conversations, not to mention a fit of the giggles when people at the Pentecostal church started falling over and lying on the floor, with the ministers in long robes speaking gibberish in loud voices and shaking their hands over them with outstretched arms."

"The really good thing was that as a trainee, Jane had to 'shadow' her supervisors, meaning that Matron couldn't tell lies about things I was supposed to have done and the doctor was never left alone with a child. I did take advantage of this to 'borrow' Alex's roller skates when he was on home leave for the weekend, and I know Matron saw me, but I never received retribution for that small sin."

"The Grove hostel for maladjusted children was closed down in the sixties, I believe, or its use changed, and it has been empty since 2004. I took my eleven plus exam there, and passed."

"You were a clever child, Julie."

"You are one of the very few people to ever have said that, Matthew."

Chapter 12

"Do you have *any* good memories of The Grove?"

"A few. My Gran had taught me to knit, and not wanting me to lose the skill, and knowing that I was a fidget and couldn't just sit still, she sent me some knitting needles, wool and a pattern for a scarf, mittens and a hat, and I was pleased to be able to knit them."

"Also, the Christmas before I left that school I had written beforehand to tell her that we were going to have a party for each class, and I had been chosen to sing in the choir to entertain everyone. She knew that I didn't have clothes of my own at the Grove – we helped ourselves to clothes from the cupboard that had been left by children who had outgrown them."

"I didn't mind that too much, but I was called into the office one Saturday morning and shown a big parcel that had arrived with my name on it. I was excited at first, then apprehensive, not believing it could be something to be happy about."

"'Well go on, then, aren't you going to open it?' Matron asked. So I opened the parcel and inside, in a pretty box and wrapped in tissue paper, was the most beautiful dress I had ever seen. It was taffeta and silk, with puffed sleeves, a stiff underskirt to make it stick out from the waist. It was royal blue with red velvet ribbon round the neck making a little bow at the front, and pearl buttons down to the waist."

"I was unable to speak, choking back tears, and Matron thought I didn't like it. She started packing it away in the box, and, scared that I would never see it again, I asked in a small voice if I could try it on and look in the mirror. She was trying to look unconcerned, but I think the dress had touched something in her and she said that of course I must try it on. And then, when the dress came out of the box, there was something else, also wrapped in tissue paper. A pair of dainty red Mary Jayne shoes. Brand new and a perfect fit."

"I was in absolute ecstasy, and put everything on, was taken to the big mirror in the hall, where I stood grinning like an idiot until the bell rang for elevenses and I had to come back to earth and change back into my ordinary clothes. But the thought of wearing that beautiful dress and those gorgeous shoes for the school party coloured my dreams and made life worth living."

"I felt like the Queen when I wore my dress at the school party, and when I sang in the choir I was moved from the back row to the front. It made me feel special, admired and beautiful and I've never since then worn anything that filled me with so much joy."

"How lovely Julie. I hope you thanked your grandma for the dress and shoes."

"Of course I did. Matron even let me use the phone to talk to Gran, and that was the only time I spoke to anyone in the family the whole time I was there."

"Did you not go home for visits?"

"No. Some of the children went home at weekends, most went home for holidays, occasionally I was the only child there. I entertained myself, read a lot of books, went out collecting walnuts from the trees in the grounds and looking for big stones to smash them open - I enjoyed eating them."

"After I learned that I had passed my eleven plus, there were discussions about sending me to Grammar School. Newark was the nearest one but was considered risky on quite a few counts. And so a decision was made ..."

Chapter 13

"You said that a decision was made. What was that decision, Julie?"

"To send me home."

"How did that make you feel?"

"Mixed feelings, Matthew. Part of me wanted to go home, start again, be really good, do what I was asked to do and put everything that happened at the Grove in a box and bury it."

"Part of me felt it would all be just the same. I would have a brother who was eight years old, who I hardly knew, and I'd be going to a new, big school with lots more children - and they might be like the children at the Grove and get me into trouble."

"As the time drew near, I felt more and more nervous and started biting my nails, often until they bled. Miss Collins noticed and put some horrid tasting ointment on them, then took me outside for a walk round the school playing field next door to the Grove."

"She told me that this would be her last week of training and she was going to move to Birmingham where she had been offered a job. I was thunderstruck as the reality of the size of the change hit home. She asked whether I was going to congratulate her, but I just shouted 'I hate you!' and ran back indoors, where I threw myself on my bed and cried my heart out. Jane came to find me and asked what was wrong."

"What was *wrong?* Everyone that I liked was taken away from me, or I was taken from them, that's what was wrong. I must be a really bad girl, mustn't I? And horrid things happen to bad girls, and I didn't know what I was going to do without Joan Collins to talk to and Joan Collins to make sense of the Strange and Horrid things. Although I knew that I would be leaving The Grove at the end of term, I hadn't really started to deal with the departure until now."

"Joan held my hand and said we were going to pray. She asked God to take me into His arms of Love and protect me from harm for as long as I lived. She taught me the Lord's Prayer, made me recite it over the next few days until I knew it, and made me promise that whenever I needed to talk to somebody about anything that bothered me, I would talk to The Lord (God). *And* that if I didn't know what to say, I could always say The Lord's Prayer."

"When she left on the Friday before my last week, I was half sad and half relieved that we couldn't say goodbye to each other. When I went to bed that evening, I pulled back the bedclothes to get my nightie and there was a card lying on top of it, which said '*God loves you, Julie.*'"

"I almost believed it."

Chapter 14

"Sit down Julie. I think we reached the time when you left The Grove last week. What happened when you went home?"

"Well, to begin with, they'd moved home. The demolition order meant that my parents received a substantial compensation for the house in Basford, which allowed them to move to Long Eaton, and I had a place at Long Eaton Grammar School. My brother had fallen out of favour and was a persistent bedwetter, so was in a remedial home in Clay Cross."

"*She* looked older and had put on a lot of weight, but she seemed okay about me coming home. The house was huge - two large rooms on the front, two bedrooms above; a porch leading into a big hall with stairs facing, and a door to the right leading to a living room and kitchen beyond. My bedroom was above the living room, which had a coal fire and back burner, so we had a warm house with a bathroom and hot water. There was a workshop on the side of the kitchen and a long garden beyond."

"My primary school term had ended two weeks before primary schools in Long Eaton, which were then governed by Derbyshire County Council. So I was sent to a girls' school, minutes away from our street. It was interesting to be with only girls, who I discovered to be quite sneaky and bitchy. We had dancing lessons, swimming lessons and music lessons, which I was not a bit keen on, although I didn't mind singing. But I was exceptionally unimpressed and also terrified when we were taken to the local swimming baths, lined up on the side in our swimsuits and pushed unceremoniously into the pool. I already had a fear of water; this enhanced that fear and I never forgave that teacher."

"The last weekend of my time at Wellington Street Girls' School I was taken into Long Eaton and kitted out with the Autumn term school uniform for Long Eaton Grammar School; bottle green gymslip and blazer plus gabardine mac and beret, white blouses and green and yellow striped tie. I didn't like green much, but the secondary school - Wilsthorpe, which was nearer - had a grey uniform and that was much worse."

"I soon realised that I was 'different' from the majority of the children in my form, 1D. For a start, my National Health specs made me stand out. There were other children who wore glasses, yes, but not round, brown, NHS ones. The other girls wore nice shoes and mine were more like clodhoppers. The girls wore their gymslips short. Mine was way past my knees."

"And finally, I was the youngest in the class,

as my birthday was in July and I was only just 11. I couldn't do anything about being the youngest, but there was a factory across the road with a wall that had gaps in it, so I would nip behind the wall, take off my specs and my shoes and bag them, put a piece of elastic round the waist of my gymslip and hike it up 6 inches, put on the shoes that I'd begged my Gran to buy - black shiny patent leather, with pointy toes - and step out again a new me."

"I enjoyed learning and was an avid reader, with a love of language and words. By this time I'd already worked my way through all the Famous Five books by Enid Blyton, Anne of Green Gables, David Copperfield and several other Dickens' novels. Now I was into Dennis Wheatley and the Dark Arts. I was more than thrilled to find that the local library was right next door to the school, and I virtually lived in that library. Every day after school I would take back yesterday's books, read one or two short stories and take home four new books, which I would read in the park. Even on my way home my nose was stuck in a book, and then from getting home to going to sleep, more reading."

"My dad had started to watch the pennies, then, numbering each sheet of toilet paper (a step up from the quartered sheets of newspaper or The Radio Times) so that he could lecture us on how much it cost, and he would turn the electricity off at 8:30 pm if my bedroom light was on and I was reading. My Grandma gave me a torch when I asked her to, and the reading continued."

"I had my lunch at school for the princely sum of 5 shillings a week and Dad had a job at the radiator factory in Long Eaton which had a canteen, so evening meals were usually bread and whatever you could find to put on it. Occasionally *she* would cook a huge heap of rock cake - or at least, that was what it looked and tasted like. It was not at all tempting and I often wondered how many flies had already shared it, since it was left out on the table, uncovered."

"Breakfast was whatever was left of the bread and whatever could be found to put on it, and I'd usually pick fruit from the garden and eat it on my way to school, or just not bother. Dad went to work at seven-thirty each morning so I often didn't see him until he came home again at night."

"Imagine my surprise, then, to wake up one mid-September morning to find Dad sitting at the table in the living room, reading the paper. I looked at him and he smiled. 'Where is *she*?' I asked."

"'She's gone to hospital,' was the reply. 'Why?'

'You'll see in a few days,' was all I got as an explanation. So I went to school and told anyone who asked that *she* had blood poisoning, and then for a couple of weeks I was taken to an old lady's house in the morning (where I was always given breakfast) and her husband would be waiting for me outside school. He walked me back to their house, about three streets away from our house, then Dad would pick me up after work and take me home. We ate quite a lot of fish and chips in those two weeks, and the neighbours brought food round, too. It was quite exciting, really."

"Then *she* came home. With a baby."

"Was this a surprise to you Julie?

"Yes, it was - for a hundred reasons. I will tell you some of them. To begin with, I knew nothing whatsoever about where babies came from. I had never been interested in babies, didn't even know *she* was pregnant. Secondly, I knew she didn't want me or Michael, so why would she want to start all over again with a new baby?"

"Nobody had told me this was going to happen and I couldn't understand why Dad seemed so pleased about it, grinning like the Cheshire cat in Alice in Wonderland. Years later when I did the sums, I realised it was the new house that had sparked the flame that led to sex and pregnancy."

"How did the new baby affect you? Was it a brother or a sister?"

"It was a baby boy, they named him William. It was the beginning of the end, for me. One day I came home to find a note on the table.

Julie,

From now on you must do all your own washing, ironing and cooking as I am too busy with the baby. You will keep your bedroom clean and tidy and if you don't do as I ask, you will pay me a fine out of your pocket money.

Mother'

"She knew that I had two shillings and sixpence - a half crown (around 12 pence in today's currency), but it paid for most of what I needed, sweets etc. This was given to me on Sunday by Grandma or Grandpa. It didn't take her long to find things to fine me for, leaving me with nothing."

Note to Julie on the table

Monday: You didn't make your bed - fine fourpence.
Tuesday: You didn't flush the toilet - fine sixpence.
Wednesday: You left the light on in the kitchen — fine threepence.

Thursday: You didn't wash your cup and plate after breakfast - fine fourpence.
Friday: You didn't wash your school uniform this week - fine one shilling.

Mother'

"Remaining pocket money - one penny; four black jacks or fruit salad sweets. Saturdays were spent at the library."

"Sunday morning I started going to the Bethel Methodist Church on Derby Road, which I passed every day on my way to and from school. There had been an event there on a weekday and I'd stuck my nose in the door out of curiosity. I was encouraged inside, given lemonade and cake, kindness and interest, and felt that these were people I could trust not to do me harm. Would I like to come to a service on Sunday morning? Yes I would. Dad would be waiting outside afterwards and we'd get the bus to Beeston."

"I never saw him go to any church service after my christening. We would get on a bus down the road, him insisting we go upstairs where he could smoke a cigarette, and I would lean this way and that avoiding the smoke which, with the exaggerated bumpiness the top deck offered, made me feel sick. We'd arrive in

Beeston and walk from the town centre or catch a green City bus to Granville Avenue, then walk round the corner to Trent Vale Road and Gran's bungalow. I would often be deathly pale and I was twig thin again, so I looked like a wraith. But once my dinner and pudding were inside me, my colour and my grin were restored. I just loved Sunday afternoons, helping Gran wash up, preparing tea, watching Captain Pugwash, The Royal Variety Show, Sunday Night at the London Palladium, The Black and White Minstrels, The Comedians, Laurel and Hardy, Charlie Chaplin, Ken Dodd, Norman Wisdom, Shari Lewis and Lamb Chop the sock puppet, and many other delights on TV."

"We only had a television in the old house once, it was borrowed and wired up for the Queen's Coronation in 1953, just two weeks before Michael was born. All the neighbours crowded inside, or stood outside, watching through the window in the back yard. It was black and white, flickering and jolty, I watched for a few minutes then toddled off to Billy Bacon's Field."

"That's a lot of memories, Julie. We'll continue next time"

Chapter 15

"You said that you felt that this time after your brother was born was the beginning of the end. What did you mean by that?"

"It started with the fines. I was okay with washing and ironing, but *she* now had most of my pocket money. Then it tipped over from the pocket money and started to be taken out of my dinner money, and I had to find excuses for not having school dinners every day."

"I also started my periods then, in a spectacular way. I knew nothing about the biology of menstruation. It was spring 1962. I was still eleven, twelve in July, and we wore green and white checked dresses in the spring and summer terms. I was leaving English class to go upstairs for a Chemistry lesson and became aware that the classmates behind me were pointing and sniggering; I supposed that somebody had stuck something on my back, as they often did - to me, especially."

"When I got to the Chemistry lab, the school Deputy Head, who was also the sick bay manager and taught domestic science (cookery and sewing), whisked me away and took me into the girls' cloakroom."

"She asked did I know what had happened? I was bemused, had absolutely no idea what she was talking about. Then she brought the back of my dress round to the front, where a large bloodstain stared back at me. I think I had some sort of a panic attack, thinking I was going to bleed to death, and making a kind of howling noise. She calmed me down and explained the process of menstruation to me. I was no longer a child but a woman, and I would have to wear a sanitary towel in my pants for a few days every month."

"I didn't *want* to be a woman, I hadn't finished being a child, and the hormones my body was generating made me feel like an *angry* child."

"The Deputy Head gave me the necessary towels and an elastic belt to hold everything in place, and a cardigan from Lost Property to cover the stain. This cardigan must be returned to the school tomorrow, she said."

"I wanted to run away, disappear, become invisible, be somebody else. I didn't need the extra washing, buying of sanitary towels, looking ridiculous at school, feeling like an alien, it was just too much."

"It was a young age to have so much to cope with, how did you do it?"

"Well, first I fell out with God and shouted at Him when I was alone and far away, on one of my long walks. I told Him He was a nasty old man for giving me a monster for a mother, a rotten life and periods. How could He say that He cares for His Children and then do this to them when He has the power to change anything bad into something good?"

"Then I stopped going to church, going instead on long walks, often to Trent Lock, about three miles away. The church people had worked on me - in a nice way - giving me lots of praise. I'd passed three bible knowledge exams with flying colours and was even teaching in the Sunday School. When one of the children, aged around four, asked me why I believed in God, it made me think very hard and I couldn't in all honesty answer the question. So I left."

"I was stealing shillings from the pile by the gas meter at home, living on bread rolls and butter - I could get quite a lot for a shilling by not having school dinners. I began writing nasty poems and stories about horrible people who came to a bad end, some of which were discovered, unfortunately, and not well received. That meant more shame, more disgrace and more fuel to add to the belief that I was a bad person."

"Having been moved up from the D stream at the Grammar School to 2B, it seemed I was brighter than I appeared to be, but I started to slide into not being able to concentrate, being late for school, absent without explanation, not doing my homework, generally having an attitude which was both disrespectful and belligerent, and badly behaved generally. I had one friend and two casual friends who were considered bad influences on me, and Ellen (the melon) and I spent many a break poking sticks into the stream which divided the school from the library, delighting in the smelly bubbles that we produced."

"It was in this pastime that we used to make plans to disrupt Physics classes. We would flick mercury down the grooves in the bench, turn on Bunsen burners, and the best trick we ever did was this: we planned out a route round the physics lab, starting at the top of the blackboard which one of us would point at to start us off, then we both followed the preset route with our eyes until the whole class - and the teacher, poor soul - were looking for something that wasn't there. Only Ellen and I were in on it. Great fun!"

"At the end of year 1 we were given a sheet of paper with two headings on it, right and left: German and Latin. We were told to circulate the paper round the class, with everyone to add their name under one heading or the other, to determine which language they would learn the next year. I chose Latin, but there were too many pupils on the Latin list, so the last six were transferred to the German list. As I sat at the back in the corner, I'd been the last to put my name on the list, so had no choice."

"I gave the German teacher (who was also 2B's form teacher) absolute Hell, giving only wrong answers to questions although I usually knew the right one. I like words and languages, but I don't like being given a choice and then having it taken away. It is amazing that now I can hold a reasonable conversation in German, having tried so hard not to learn the language!"

"So, Julie, you became a rebel!"

Chapter 16

"Well, Julie 'the rebel'. Let's hear how that went, shall we?"

"Like everything else, Matthew, it went badly. *She* caught me stealing shillings from the pile by the meter one morning. *She* grabbed my arm, swung me round, then let go, and I smashed into the kitchen wall and fell over. I ran out of the house and down three streets to the doctor's surgery. Dr Frost had seen me several times, because I'd had urinary tract infections, missed periods and painful bleeding, so he knew me a little."

"I was crying and hurting, and when the receptionist said I would have to wait until the end of surgery to see the doctor, I wailed until she gave in and showed me into his consulting room after the previous patient came out."

"I told him what had happened and he looked at the bruises which were beginning to show, checked that nothing was broken and told me that it was very wrong to steal, especially from your parents. So I told him why I had to do it. He was very quiet for a while, walking up and down behind his desk, contemplating."

"Then he said that hurting me was also very wrong and violence never put any wrong right. He made a phone call while I waited in the waiting room. Afterwards, he told me that his wife had asked him if they could find someone to mind their baby girl this morning, as she had some things she needed to do, so would I be so kind as to go to his house and help Mrs Foster? He wrote his address on a piece of paper. It was only round the corner from our house, and although babies were not my favourite choice of things to look after, anything was better than having to go back home or to school in the state I was in."

"After he'd seen his last patient of the morning, the doctor went round to our house and told *her* that he had informed the school as to why I was absent … and I don't know what else he said, but he did say that I had been helping his wife with their little girl, that they were pleased with me and would be asking me to help regularly, out of school hours of course. He collected me from his house after a few words with Madeleine, his wife, then took me home, waited while I gathered up my school stuff, and then drove me to school in his car."

"That made me feel a bit special, even more different, and grateful. I babysat quite often at weekends and occasional evenings or straight after school, and he was a lovely man with a lovely wife and a cute little girl that I became fond of. I had a protector!"

"Not for long, though. Because *she* couldn't carry on fining me, hurting me or neglecting me, she started beating up Dad after I was in bed. He never put up any resistance, which must have been frustrating for her. I had to lie awake and hear this going on, all the while wishing that he would defend himself, or whack her back at least and tell her to STOP IT!"

"Then *she* started taking it out on my Grandma, writing vitriolic letters, issuing threats that anything Gran bought for me would be dust-binned, saying that her boys would never see their grandmother so they couldn't be brain-washed by her, and more. I have some of those letters, Matthew, and I will read them to you one day, so you get her perspective on things."

"How come the letters are in your possession, Julie?"

"My dad had just about had enough, the constant tension between his wife and his mother was doing his head in, and he had begun to consider divorce. I was nearly 13 and was aware of this, being caught up in the middle as it were. Grandma kept the letters as evidence that my dad was married to a psychopath."

"Hang on, Julie - did your grandma say that?"

"No, of course she didn't Matthew, that's my take on it, but Granny did keep the letters.

They were brought into the court as evidence and the divorce was granted, but it took him two years to get the Decree Nisi."

"Then the letters were passed to Enid, his first girlfriend, who was now back in a relationship with him, her first husband having died. Enid gave them to me when Dad died some years later."

"Of course, I felt that it was my fault they got divorced. I was a thief and a horrible person, and if I had never been born, none of this would have happened."

A frown crossed Matthew's forehead and he sat up, leaned forward and put his hand up, palm facing outwards.

"Stop right there, Julie. NONE of this was your fault. Your mother had problems and was not able to deal with you. She may have had postnatal depression or any number of issues arising from her own childhood. She should have asked for help and your father should have supported her instead of giving in to her violence. In no way was their problem *your* fault, you must remember that. Use it as your mantra for moving forward, beginning to like yourself and getting on with your life, Julie."

"Yes, Matthew, I know the theory of liking myself. I've seen quite a few head-doctors since 'the incident' and convinced them that I know what I have to do. But I have never been able to convince myself."

"We have a few more things to cover before we are ready to talk about 'the incident', Julie. How do you feel right now?"

"I have stirred up some bad feelings today, Matthew, but I'll go home and look at the photo albums of my children and that will make me feel better. Next week we can talk about Castle Hill."

"I look forward to that, Julie. Now, off you go for some photo therapy."

Chapter 17

"Hello Julie, sit down. You said we could talk about Castle Hill today?"

"Yes Matthew, but we have to look at the events that got me there first."

"I was in a very bad place - literally and metaphorically - when I was 12. My form was going to spend a week in the Lake District, in a youth hostel in Bassenthwaite, and I was going with them. I don't know who paid for it but I didn't care, I was going to escape. Apart from the journey, when the bus had to stop several times both ways for me to be sick, the week was glorious."

"We climbed the three highest peaks, Scafell Pike, Helvellyn and Skiddaw, and a few more, and had midnight feasts. We had a whale of a time, and for the first time since I said goodbye to the gypsies, I felt like I was part of something and fitted in."

"When we climbed Helvellyn there was great excitement. As we set off back from the summit along Striding edge, the weather changed drastically, from cloudy and cool to stormy and snowing, and we were all quite scared, even the teachers. We all huddled together as best we could on the narrow path under an overhang of rock, where we waited for half an hour for the weather to improve."

"When it didn't, we were tied in a line with a rope, with one adult to two children. I was linked with a German fellow - Hans something - and a boy called Christopher, and we set off very slowly, with Hans calling out every few yards to check we were okay. He got us playing word games, singing -

'Ach du lieber Augustin, Augustin Augustin,
ach du lieber Augustin alles ist hin.
Gelt ist weg Mäd'l ist weg, Alles hin, Augustin.
Ach, du lieber Augustin,
Alles ist hin.
Rock ist weg, Stock ist weg,
Augustin liegt im Dreck,
Ach, du lieber Augustin,
Alles ist hin.'"

"There were a lot more verses, and if I had known at that time what the song was about, (the Plague) I might well have thrown myself off Striding Edge! Hans taught us more songs, word games which helped to keep our spirits up, and he was so kind that, naturally, I fell in love with him, and when we got back to the hostel I followed him around like a puppy dog, getting him to show me how to play chess and generally mooning about, dreaming dreams of castles in Austria, happy ever after and all that goes with teenage crushes. I made some enquiries, not very subtly, and discovered he was with our school on an exchange of some sort for one term, so that would be another goodbye for me."

"To get back to the tale of Helvellyn, when we finally got off the mountain it was dusk and there were vehicles, lights and people coming towards us with blankets and hot drinks, and boy what a relief that was. The hostel manager had contacted the mountain rescue team when we weren't back at the hostel at the appointed time, and the rest is obvious. When the time came to leave the Lakes I was not just sad, I was devastated. I had been happy all week, and when I thought about what was waiting for me at home, I couldn't face it."

"As I came through the door *she* was shouting at Dad, pushing him round the living room table with one hand, a frying pan in the other, her face screwed up in hatred and anger, and I started screaming. I couldn't stay in this hell hole, I had to do something. When that happens, like many other people I look at fight or flight. I couldn't think of any more ways to fight *her*, and I couldn't stand her constant chipping away at me, punishing me - mentally, since Dr Frost had put an end to the physical abuse. Dad was getting the physical abuse now and that was the last straw. I spent the weekend in my bedroom, too miserable to do anything but read."

"After school on Monday I found another note on the table - meant for my dad to read, but he had left it on the table."

20.02.63

Julie offered to do some shopping on her way back from school today, so thinking it would be something useful for her to do I gave her a list and money.

She came back on the bus, brought the wrong thing for 2 of the 6 items, 'borrowed' a shilling without asking, said she had bought a coffee and a cake in town (most likely her real reason for going).

This has happened many times before, always when she has spent all her pocket money. Then she woke Billy up when she came back. He had been asleep in his pram in the hall for 20 minutes.

"I was incensed. *SHE* had taken all my pocket money, plus two days' dinner money, and this had been an attempt to get some back to buy sanitary towels. *That* was the 'coffee and cake', which I *didn't* have."

"So, leaving the note on the table, I put some food into my little bucket bag and left home. I had no real plan, but I thought I'd walk as far as I could, then find somewhere to sleep - a bus shelter or a barn. Then I'd just keep walking till I had a better plan. I'd put on my warmest clothes, and after eating the fruit and bread I wasn't hungry. I walked along the canal towards Ilkeston and several times thought I might jump in the canal, but couldn't do it because of the deep water phobia. It was dark by the time I left the canal, and half a mile down the main road I suddenly thought about hitching a ride. Quite a few lorries had passed me by, and I thought that if I stuck out my thumb, one might stop."

"So I did, and after some thirty or more vehicles had passed, a lorry indicated and pulled up, the driver winding his window down and asking, 'where yer goin' luv?' He was opening the passenger door, so I climbed up into the cab, and he moved off."

"He was looking at me a bit strangely, then he repeated the question. I had no idea what to say, I hardly knew which way I was facing, so I said that wherever he was going was fine by me. He looked a bit perplexed, but carried on driving."

"I woke up when he pulled into an all-night truckers café and wondered where we were. He said we were stopping as he needed a hot drink, and he would get one for me. I said I had no money, but he said that was okay, he would pay for it. We went inside and I sat down, and he brought coffee for himself and hot chocolate for me. He stared at me until I got fidgety, then asked me how old I was. I said 16, and he asked why I was out so late, on my own, hitching lifts from strangers, and did I know how dangerous that was?"

"I began to panic, then - I had seen reports in the papers about girls going missing and ending up dead. My panic must have been obvious, because he said not to worry, he wasn't going to hurt me. The question came again - why was I out late at night etc etc? I ended up blurting out the whole story, and he listened. It was only when he reached out and put his hand on my shoulder that I gave in to the tears, which poured out like a burst dam. There were only two other people in the café, and in spite of the fact they were staring at us, I clung to this stranger until the hurt melted away and only my body was left, wracked and shaken."

"He said he was going to take me home and sort it out with my parents, and I thought that if he was there, I'd be okay."

"He got me back into the lorry, gave me a blanket which was itchy and smelt oily, but which

107

warmed me up and stopped me shaking, and about an hour later we were back at Canal Street."

"He rang the bell, and my dad came to the door. He was so relieved to see me that he cried, then told me off for causing him to be so worried. It was twenty-past eleven. He told me to get off to bed when the man asked if he could come in and talk to them."

"I fell asleep listening to the three of them talking about what had happened. I felt bad, because I hadn't even asked him his name, never mind thanking him for helping me."

"My dad didn't go to work next day and I didn't go straight to school either. He said I was bloody lucky that a decent Christian man had picked me up, and not a man like the ones in the papers who could have raped and murdered me without a second thought. It was only five months later that the notorious Moors Murderers claimed their first victim."

"For once, my dad was decisive. He went with me to the school and spoke to the headmaster, who said the school had contacted the Child Welfare Department after Dr Frost had informed them of his concerns. They had been about to call us in to discuss my behaviour and downhill progress at school."

"Within days we heard that a place was available for me at two Derbyshire boarding schools - one in Buxton and one in Bakewell. I was to choose."

"How did you feel about that, Julie?"

"Excited, nervous, relieved, sad, joyful - all of these feelings in quick succession. And then disbelief. A choice. I could choose! I had never had any say in my life and my future - this was completely overwhelming."

"And it meant I could escape from HER!"

Chapter 18

"Hello Julie. That was quite a session last week. I hope you've had a good rest?"

"Yes Matthew, and I'm finding it cathartic to open up memories in order to close the book finally."

"Hmmm. So which school did you choose?"

"Lady Manners School, Bakewell. In a matter of days, I was packed and ready to go. When I say packed, I had very little and had been told that I would be fully kitted out when I arrived at the boarding house - at great expense no doubt, according to Dad."

"Dad had taken me to see Gran to say goodbye, and I jumped for joy when she said that she and Gramps would be able to visit me there and bring Dad, too, and that my pocket money would be given to me on Saturday morning every week, come what may."

"I went on the train, as I wasn't a good traveller on buses, and was met at Bakewell station by Mrs Hodges, the wife of the Geography teacher at the school, who was responsible for the running of the boarding house – Castle Hill. We walked down Station Road, turned right, and just a few steps took us to the gate and the path up to the main building of the house. This was the girls' block; the boys' block was a newer concrete construction to the right, separated from the main building by a pond. It was a beautiful old house with a stable block, built in the late 18th century and with many additions and alterations since, but had maintained a homely feel. And I felt very much at home in it."

"It closed to boarders in 2003, and the last time I went to look at it, in 2015, it was being used as a conference centre. It's now a Grade II listed building, which was renovated, sold as one residence in 2016 and recently turned into flats."

"The name Castle Hill was appropriate as there had been a small mott and bailey castle higher up, which was excavated in the 1970's."

"I was shown where I would be sleeping, the dining room, the games room, where the boarders could play table tennis, listen to the radio or play records. Then the kitchen and the laundry room. Everything I would need to know was explained to me, what time breakfast was eaten, what time homework was done (in the dining room) and how there would be a buzzer which would announce when it was time to be somewhere and do something."

"When the boarders came back from school I was nervous about meeting them. I didn't know what kind of child went to boarding school and from the books I'd read I had a half-baked impression it was only rich people that sent their children there. It turned out that I was partly right and very much wrong. As there was a fee involved, some of the parents were well off. Some - indeed half - of the parents were in the Armed forces in places like Singapore and Aden, and boarding school was considered better for all involved than an education abroad, around the instability of a forces life, with its frequent upheaval and moving home."

"Several children were the unfortunate victims of the breakdown of family relations, or wards of court, and some were there because the school had a good reputation, and a good education was a much sought after prize in the 1960's."

"Then there was me, a maladjusted child whose mother didn't want her, whose father wouldn't or couldn't protect her anymore, and whose fees were to be paid by what is now Social Services and was known then as the Child Welfare Department."

"I almost fitted in, and I was not going to behave badly in case they sent me home!"

"I was taken to Broughtons, the shop in Bakewell that sold Lady Manners' School uniform, on my first morning. (It also sold lovely leisure wear and was quite posh). There, I was treated like a real Lady. They kitted me out with the uniform, plus underwear, socks, nightwear and bras. I didn't *want* a bra and I made a fuss, but was told that a bra was necessary and a part of the school uniform, so I gave in."

"The uniform was very smart, navy, with an A-line skirt - altered while we shopped - so that when I was kneeling down the hem touched the floor. The white blouse and navy tie were an improvement on the green I was used to. Summer uniform was a short sleeved full-skirted gingham dress, with or without a navy cardigan. Mine was red, as were all the boarders in Glossop house. Cockerton house was yellow, Barker green and Taylor sky blue."

"Lady Manners School began on 20 May 1636. This was when Grace, Lady Manners, set up a fund to pay a teacher and wrote a set of rules to guide the initial stages of the school. It opened properly the next year. It was a charity school to provide free education for poor boys in Bakewell and Rowsley. The School Charter from 1636 still exists and confirms these arrangements. I believe the houses were named after local landowners who had contributed to funding and projects at the school."

"I had never had so many new clothes! I was also allowed to choose some recreational wear, which made me feel very special, and (I'm told) made my father go pale and almost pass out when he was sent the bill. I also had my own towels and was given name tapes later to stitch into all my new kit."

"Then, in my new uniform I was taken to school in the afternoon."

"Bakewell is such a beautiful town. The school was right at the top of the town with fields for miles around, and most of the children came in buses from the nearby villages. Hulley's buses were legendary - rattly, bumpy and smelling of teenagers. They mostly got you to your destination, though, come rain, snow, floods and wind."

"The school itself was local stone, much prettier than the red brick of Long Eaton Grammar School and, of course, the air was fresh. I threw myself into learning and was proud that I was ahead of my year in French. I was moved to the top set. Unfortunately, I was also put in the top set for maths, where I floundered until it was noted that I was copying from the girl beside me, who, unfortunately, was no better than me. We both moved down a set, with the teacher of Set 2 not up to the task of teaching and ending up having a nervous breakdown."

"Whatever did you do to her, Julie?"

"Nothing, Matthew. Well, no more than any other pupil who could see ways and means to get through 40 minutes of maths without actually doing any mathematics! I was doing okay, though. Not too skilled where science was concerned, but I was able to drop those subjects the following year, to study for O-levels."

"My form teacher in my last year was also the Religious Instruction teacher, and he greatly encouraged me to use the knowledge I had gained from Sunday School attendance to make sense of the Bible, and to debate issues with skill. I joined the debating society at school and was thoroughly at home discussing topics that were of interest, even when I had to adopt a view and win a debate when it was not my actual point of view. That has helped me to see things from other perspectives throughout my life, and is a valuable asset."

"Yes, you're right Julie. You have a certain eloquence which is easy, yet well-informed, and your experiences have taught you not to be judgemental until you know all of the facts."

"Thank you, Matthew. You're a good listener. I'll stop there as the next episode will take some putting together. I might have to write it down and ask you to read it before we meet next week."

"That's fine Julie, we'll do it however is best for you."

"Thanks, Matthew. 'Bye now."

Chapter 19

Hello Matthew, I have written this for you.

I liked most of the teachers at Lady Manners. They all had lots of positive qualities, some had a sense of humour and some struggled to cope with the boundless energy and trickery we possessed as teenagers. I did have to write some short dissertations on, for instance, 'the dangers of arriving at school on time' and 'the hazards of placing objects on top of half open doors,' but none of my naughtiness was malicious and no worse than most pupils - although I was probably more daring, impulsive and fearless than the majority, and I quite enjoyed writing.

One teacher I could not stand was the Biology teacher. He was a self-professed atheist, constantly mocking the Bible and its contents, making us write passages from it and tearing them up and binning them without even glancing at them, if we committed offences such as not paying attention, not handing in homework on time, talking in class, etc. He was also sleazy and looked at certain of the girls as if he knew them more intimately than was professional or acceptable.

In class, we had covered dissection of eyes and hearts of animals and were embarking on human reproduction. While most of the girls kept their heads down and squirmed with embarrassment, most of the boys were snorting and making rude gestures for the sake of bravado. Mr Sherley gave us the details of sexual intercourse winking at the boys and obviously enjoying the girls' discomfort.

I wrote it all down.
Then I stopped breathing and felt dizzy.
Then nauseous.
Then I threw up on my exercise book.

'Oh it's not that bad, Julie, you might even enjoy it,' said Mr Sherley.

I don't know how I did it, but I ran out of the lab, across the playing field and collapsed, breathless and faint, by the dry stone wall. My mind had travelled back to the Grove, the room, the chair, the cane, the Doctor, me, my pants round my ankles. It wasn't the cane he was shoving inside my vagina ...

So there you have it, Matthew, that was when my world fell apart and nothing was ever the same again. Not only was I maladjusted, bad, unlovable and unwanted, I had been forced to surrender my childhood without even knowing it at the time. He had stolen something that could never be reclaimed. I wanted to die.

When the search party found me, they took me to the school sick bay and sent a classmate to fetch my satchel and blazer from the Biology lab. I stayed in the sick bay till home time, when one of the senior boarders came to walk back to Castle Hill with me. I didn't speak for two days, just nodding my head when questioned, and couldn't eat either. I went over everything in my head, knowing that I couldn't share this with ANYBODY. Not even my Gran. Especially not my Gran.

I felt dirty, ugly, stupid, angry. Why had I allowed it to happen? Eventually, when I realised that I had been powerless, a child, with only the knowledge of a child, I realised that although it would always be with me, I had to bury that event so deep in my subconscious that I could go forward as if nothing had happened.

Of course, subconscious knowledge has ways of manifesting itself, often in dreams, and I started to have horrible dreams and would wake the girls in the dorm up with my moaning and groaning, sometimes calling out and talking. Generally, they would just say, 'shut up Julie!' and I would go back to sleep.

I will leave it there Matthew. See you next week.

Julie

Chapter 20

"Hello Julie. I've read your letter, and I found it very disturbing. The abuse has obviously affected you deeply, and I'm sure it's been something very difficult to come to terms with. I have to say that you are a survivor. I believe that the trauma you survive makes you stronger in the end, and although it may not seem that way, you've dealt successfully with what life has thrown at you and gained wisdom from the experiences you survived."

I felt a rush of anger coursing through my brain - the sudden thought that something I had experienced as non-sexual had in fact been sexual. I tried to banish it, failed, and yelled at Matthew.

"YOU DON'T KNOW THE HALF OF IT, Matthew! I'm sorry to shout at you, but you've touched a raw nerve telling me that!"

"I'm sorry, Julie. It was meant to be reassuring. Just begin when you are ready, and I will wait and listen."

"Okay, I can move on, now. I didn't move on back then, though. There was a fiery ball of anger deep inside me that threatened to explode and burn down everything around me. I became sullen, careless and uncooperative with the adults that crossed my path. I felt as if my peer group knew all about me and despised me. I didn't want any friends, because even if they did happen to like me, they would disappear from my life just like every friend I'd ever made in the past had done. I was very much alone. All adults were untrustworthy. I had somehow forgotten Jane Collins, Dr Frost, the lorry driver, my old neighbour Mrs Brown and the school caretaker who had observed me rummaging in the dustbins for food. My gran was the only person I could trust and I could never tell her what the doctor had done."

"I went home for the first Boarder's weekend, leaving on Friday after school and returning Sunday evening. When I arrived, my dad wasn't there. *She* said he was in his shop, on Bennet Street. I didn't want to have a conversation about it with *her* so I went off to find Dad and his shop."

"He told me that he had started divorce proceedings, bought the shop, and was living above it. It was a newsagents/tobacconists, with small stocks of items like baked beans, sweets and chocolate, not much at all. It was shabby and badly in need of a good clean and refurbishment, a lick of paint and some furniture. He seemed cheerful enough, enjoyed his trips to the wholesaler and conversations with the few people who came into the shop, mainly Asians and Afro-Caribbeans who had moved into the streets in that part of Long Eaton."

"I asked if I could stay with him and help out with the shop, washing and cleaning, but he said there was no bed or furniture apart from what was in his room, so I went back to Canal Street. I picked up my suitcase from the hall and was about to sneak upstairs to my bedroom, but *she* was waiting for me and told me that I would be sleeping in the garden in a tent, as she had rented out the three bedrooms to casual workers in the area who needed accommodation."

"I was dumbfounded. I just looked at her in disbelief. I thought briefly about going back to Bakewell, but knew that it would cause trouble. I considered going to Beeston on the bus and staying with Grandma, but knew that would cause even more trouble, and in any case, I felt too fragile to be able to hold my emotions in check."

"So I slept in a tent in the garden for two nights. Every emotion was whirling around my head as I lay under the stars. The initial anger at being treated like a dog became self-pity. *Why* was I so bad, so unlovable? If I died in the night, would *she* just leave me there for the Council to remove with the rubbish on bin day? Why was I worth nothing to *her*? Sadness - was I ever going to be loved? Despair - why would anybody want to care anyway? Everything that was good in my life would be taken away - I didn't deserve anything better."

"Resolution - I was never going to see *her* face EVER again. She had performed her last act of unkindness to me and it was over. I meant it with every fibre of my being."

"I spent Saturday in the library. Sunday I spent with Dad and Sunday late afternoon I went back to Castle Hill, hungry and tired and determined that that would be the last time I ever went back to Long Eaton."

Chapter 21

"Back at Castle Hill I began to unwind. The food at the boarding house was mediocre. Cooked food - burst boils (watered down cheese) on toast was to be avoided, but cold food - sandwiches, salads and biscuits — were not to be despised. We took some leftover Christmas cake to the boys' block one January evening - we were allowed there until 8 pm at weekends under supervision of the boys' housemaster, and would normally watch Dr Who after Top of the Pops there, nibbling Blue Riband chocolate wafer biscuits, but this particular evening, to our indignation and sorrow, the TV was out of order. We were out for revenge and took turns in throwing the cake at the plaster over the door lintel, dissolving in fits of laughter when the plaster fell off the wall and the cake remained intact. We also got into trouble later, when the fish in the pond were dying and the cause was found to be cereal boxes full of cooked breakfast and suppers which were smuggled out of the dining room and unceremoniously dumped in the pond."

"Fortunately, the lunches at school, cooked in a splendid kitchen serving the main hall, were excellent. I have fond memories of steak and kidney pie with pastry that was halfway between flaky and shortcrust, fish pie with delicious white sauce and cheesy topped mashed potato, cottage pie was minced beef and shepherd's pie was minced lamb – and you knew them apart. Vegetables were crisp, even cabbage, no lingering smells of overcooking, and the puddings were divine. Their pet names were far from appetising, but the taste was sublime. Dead fly pie, concrete jam, frogspawn and blood, Poo pie and scab and matter pudding, otherwise known as Mince tart, jam roly poly, sago with jam, chocolate pie and trifle, along with treacle sponge, Manchester tart (jam and coconut), Neapolitan slice and other glorious desserts were on offer and remain fixed in my memory to this day."

"As time went on, I had metamorphosed from a skinny wraith into a healthy and well-proportioned 15 year old. Only my face was unaware of the changes. My periods had resumed, regular and painful, and I was carried out of the assembly hall on a monthly basis having passed out on the oak parquet-tiled floor. We were still a religious nation in 1965, so each day began with prayers, a hymn, notices, and inspection as we entered the Assembly Hall - also the Dining Hall."

"The boys were inspected by Ponty - Mr Bridges, from Wales - who would pick random boys, say 'elevate your trousers, boyo' and check they were wearing standard uniform socks."

"Miss Wheeler, short and stout with very little hair that was twisted into a knot on top of her very round head, would stop any girl with her hair loose, taking hold of the hair saying 'what's this girlie? Tie it up or I will cut it off!'"

"My friend Harriet and I wore our hair long. Hers was beautiful golden blond, thick and slightly wavy, and after Miss Wheeler had made her a victim, she came to school one day and we all fell about laughing. She had plaited her hair around a piece of coat-hanger, formed into a half swastika, pointing up one side and down the other. She walked right past Miss Wheeler, who was apoplectic and purple with rage, but had no legitimate claim to arrest her as it was tied up."

"When it was school photo time, as the camera roved in a semicircle round the class, the girls would quickly pull elastics, ribbons, hairgrips and other restrictions from their hair, replacing them once the picture was taken. There was always a huge queue outside Miss Wheeler's office when the photographs were delivered!"

"Having said all that, Miss Wheeler taught me French and did a sterling job - though had I been unable to rattle off declensions, remember tenses and adjectival endings, I too would have been one of the many made to stand on their chair when they got something wrong."

Chapter 22

"When Granny was unable to have me for weekends and holidays, I stayed at Castle Hill."

"Quite often there'd be other boarders there who had no relatives in the UK and couldn't travel abroad to their parents for some reason or other. I had joined the local library in the first week I was in Bakewell and was a regular bookworm, and when there *was* nobody else staying on, I spent my time reading or banging a tennis ball against the wall which held up the Mound at the back of the house."

"The pocket money my grandparents were supplying was paid out on Saturday mornings and we were allowed into Bakewell in groups of four to spend it."

"I was, at last, able to buy pretty much anything I wanted as well as things that I needed, and quite often my group would go into the Parrakeet, a coffee bar on Church Lane, and pretend to be 'groovy'. We would listen to records on the juke box and argue which group was better - the Beatles or the Rolling Stones, Cliff Richard or Elvis Presley, Dusty Springfield or Petula Clark."

"We were so privileged to be teenagers in the sixties, when it was all happening on the arts scene, especially the music. Sadly, we didn't appreciate it then, and we were all battling with the hormones that made our moods swing as much as the music. I became a big fan of the Beach Boys and started my collection, which I still have and now stands at around 30 LP's and some singles and EP's. When I feel my mood's getting low I always listen to the Beach Boys and it lifts me out of it."

"I would fall asleep listening to the sound of the River Wye as it burbled over the stones, thinking of the trout which were very much a presence. Often I'd read a book under the covers by torchlight, or listen to radio Caroline, praying that we would not be discovered and the radio confiscated. The Top of the Pops program was what we lived for. It was really hard not to sing along, but that was a risk too far."

"A new girl arrived who was to share the dormitory with myself, Lydia and Maxine. Her name was Lisa, she had frizzy blondish hair and was shy. She would get dressed and undressed under her dressing gown and we teased her quite a lot about it, asking if she had some kind of deformity, and staring at her to see if we could see what the deformity was, playing guessing games."

"I suppose we were quite mean, and she often burst into tears. Then we would have to try extra hard to make her laugh, so that the housemistress didn't come to find out what was wrong. One night, she was snivelling into her pillow, and we asked what she was crying for."

"She missed her brother, she said. Something possessed me to tell her that I had five brothers, so I should be crying five times harder than she was crying. It shut her up, but I then had to make up names and birthdays for three brothers I didn't have."

"The story was so good that it went round year 4 and to Harriet, who lived in Grindleford, did actually have five siblings and who immediately felt that maybe we had a few things in common. She was the one school friend that I made and have kept to this day, even though she married a German and now lives in Scotland. We had a good time as friends and shared lots of adventures, mainly skiving off Maths class and playing tennis on the field. She and her family did eventually learn the truth about my brothers, but it made no difference to our friendship."

"My life had settled into some kind of a pattern; I was clean and cared for, my needs were taken care of and I should have been happy. Instead, I roller-coastered from blissful joy into deep black quicksands of emptiness, often dreaming that I was seriously ill or dying, usually both. The only satisfaction, if it could be seen as such, was that in these dreams my parents were in bits because they had treated me so badly. They stood round my deathbed begging me to forgive them and in my nightmares, I had no voice to either forgive them or tell them they deserved to suffer."

"The nights of effortless flight were few and far between. I was rude and nasty to the other girls for no reason and they had begun to shun me. I didn't blame them, but I couldn't stop myself being horrible. It was as if I was living out the version of me that had made me unwanted."

"This was me - Julie aged 14 years and 7 months."

Chapter 23

"When the boarding house was empty, I spent a lot of time up on the Mound, an area where the castle had once stood and the icehouse was the only complete building left standing in evidence."

"If it was fine I would take a book. At the time I was fascinated by D H Lawrence, probably influenced by the media excitement caused by the publication of 'Lady Chatterley's Lover', which I had read under the desk in German lessons at Long Eaton Grammar School in 1962. It wasn't his best work – 'The Rainbow' and 'Sons and Lovers' were, in my opinion, much better works, and 'The Plumed Serpent' became my favourite of his books."

"I would sit on a tree stump under the huge oak on the Mound and read. If I was too fidgety to read I would make daisy chains, or gather leaves and grasses and make pictures with them. Sometimes I just cried. I made myself a coffin out of branches and grass one day and lay in it, quiet and still - seeing if I could make myself die, wondering what it felt like to leave the world behind. Then, realising that it would just be the same, that nobody would miss me, made me cry all the more, as loud as I liked, as nobody would hear me."

"One day I was on my knees, face almost on the ground, practicing howling like a wolf. It was the best representation of the way that I felt and I gave it my all. Wailing on the high notes and groaning on the low notes, I could almost imagine hunting with the pack, creeping up on gazelles, who leapt high and far, startled by the stealth of our approach. Then carefully scanning the immediate surroundings for evidence of lions, tigers, panthers, SNAKES ..., then 'Yoowwll!'"

"Suddenly I was aware that someone was speaking. I turned over to a sitting position, feeling very stupid and embarrassed, to see who was there, and found the boys' housemaster looking down at me with a very strange look on his face, asking me if I was in pain. I wanted the Mound to really open up and swallow me, and having run out of words, just shook my head."

"Mr Ritchie, the boys' housemaster and my former top set maths teacher, was silent for a minute or two, whilst *I* was searching my head for some kind of escape or, at worst, an explanation."

"Sudden inspiration – 'My rabbit died!' I said. The thought of rabbits dying, in particular *my* rabbit, brought me close to tears, and I kept focussing on that image to save me from further explanation. Mr Ritchie's face softened, he pointed to the tree stumps under the oak and said we could sit down and talk about my rabbit, as it would make me feel better to share it. The last thing I wanted to do was talk. To a teacher. But I told him about Hoppy, how I rescued him when his mother abandoned him when he broke his leg running away from a fox (so the vet had surmised) and how my dad built him a big hutch; how his leg mended and he had a happy, if lonely life. What I didn't tell him was that the last time I saw Hoppy, he was, true to his name, hopping around and very much alive."

"Mr Ritchie asked why I wasn't at home, with my family. I didn't know what to say in reply so, in a fit of boldness and wanting to turn the focus from myself, I said 'I could ask you the same question.'"

"He laughed then, and I recalled that I had seen him with the sixth formers, obviously sharing some comic moment or joke and thinking he was very juvenile for a teacher, although it was hard to say how old he was. His hair was going thin on top and he had one of those faces that would always look youthful, no wrinkles except for the laughter lines round his eyes. His eyes, I suddenly realised, were exactly the same colour as mine."

"I was getting up, having thought of an excuse to flee, when he said, 'I'm here because I choose to be here.' I looked him in the eye and said, 'well, I also chose to be here - at least, my Gran and Granpa are on holiday with family they haven't seen in a while, and here is the next best place. Anyway, I have to go now, I have homework to do.'"

"'Julie, I want you to promise me something before you go.'"

"Alarmed, I looked around to see if anyone was there in case I needed help. Silly, really, I knew there were just the two of us - even the boarding house staff were gone and the teachers at school teaching."

"'It's nothing to be afraid of,' he said. 'I just want you to promise that if ever you feel sad, or hurt or afraid, you will tell someone. Talk about it. It's not good for you to have these feelings and bottle them up. Talk to an adult. I will always listen if you need to talk. Okay?'"

"'Okay,' I flung over my shoulder, halfway down the mound, my heart banging in my chest like a drum. Oh God, how embarrassing was *that*?"

"I went to the dorm, got my book - a Dickens' novel - and took it to the games room, where I sat in solitude trying to concentrate on the words till cook came to tell me supper was ready; I could bring the tray back here if I liked."

"I liked."

"I took the tray back after eating the soup and roll, a cheese sandwich, an apple and a couple of biscuits, then took myself off to bed with the radio and my book. I couldn't concentrate on reading as I was intrigued by Mr Ritchie's offer, but suspicious at the same time. Nobody had ever asked me to make a promise before. I drifted off to sleep and woke briefly when the noise the radio was making told me it was time to switch it off and get back to sleep."

Chapter 24

"The rest of the weekend was spent finishing the Dickens novel. His works never failed to show me how dismal life could be in a capital city, with its squalor, deprivation for the poor and so many people working hard yet never raising themselves beyond subsistence level. The workhouse was where great numbers of women spent their last days, often with their children. If the husband had died, left the family home, or become too ill to work, poverty led desperate people to do desperate things. It intrigued me, and at the same time made me feel such pity and sadness for his characters, and I wondered why readers would actually read such novels, and become depressed by them. I didn't really understand depression then. At 15, it was not something I had even got a word for."

"Life at the boarding house resumed its routine. I tried to be content with my lot. Just fitting in was my goal, and I completely obliterated the encounter on the Mound from my memory."

"I thought Mr Ritchie had probably done the same, but if ever he saw me on my own, at school or at the boarding house, he would give me a very small nod of the head; and if I looked at him, I got a very small smile – though nothing like the great guffaws he would share with the sixth formers."

"So I couldn't blank him, although if I saw him first, I would about turn and scoot off in the opposite direction."

"My dorm-mates Lydia and Maxine and even Lisa were starting to show signs of interest in the opposite sex, and I would listen to their whispered chats after lights out, mainly with amusement. It was all I could do to keep quiet when I realised which boys they were talking about and I had to stuff the pillow case in my mouth to stop the laughter from escaping. It was mainly the boys at the boarding house, and believe me, there was only one boy boarder who was anything to write home about. He was completely attached to a fifth form girl who lived in Baslow and was probably the most attractive girl in school."

"If we had pocket money to cover it, we were occasionally allowed to go to the pictures in Bakewell on a Saturday night, usually under supervision. Lydia and Maxine would be on tenterhooks all week, planning outfits, hair makeovers, makeup and perfume. I looked forward to them coming home from the 'flea pit' and hearing about which boy's hand had been allowed up their jumper, who had been snogging who, and 'did you see Stephanie Wright? That feller she was with had his hand up her skirt!' I thought the whole business was just disgusting and a waste of time and emotion, but if they enjoyed it, so be it."

"However, there were gardeners employed by the boarding house who came in pairs, usually an experienced older man and a younger in-training youth. Women didn't take up gardening as a career in the sixties, or if they did, never usually advertised it. When I was 15 a young man named James was the trainee gardener, tall, dark haired, blue eyed, shy, sensitive and interesting. I came across him as I returned from school, just as he was planting out some tall orange flowers, and as he looked up, I asked him if they were Crocosmia. He blushed, looked at his feet, hesitated and said he wasn't sure, he would have to ask the boss."

"I felt guilty then, as I had obviously caused him embarrassment, and hurried off, not expecting to hear any more on the subject of flowers and determined not to bother him again. I was merely showing off, as my Gran had them in her garden and she had educated me on the names of many plants and flowers."

"A couple of weeks went by, different gardeners, different plants, then the man who had come with James reappeared. He told me that I was right about the Crocosmia, and I told him about my Gran's garden. We chatted for a while and then, as I was about to go, heaving my satchel back over my shoulder, he told me that James had been transferred to parks and gardens as that would give him a wider experience, so I wouldn't be seeing him again."

"I was a bit disappointed, but then a bit relieved too. I had no interest whatsoever in the boys in my year, or even lower sixth formers, perhaps one or two upper sixth formers were slightly more appealing, but the workers who drove past us on the walk up to school made me smile when they hooted and wolf-whistled at us girls in our hiked up skirts that were duly lowered before the encounter with Miss Wheeler."

"So I was lost for words when the gardener gave me a piece of paper with a phone number on it! He told me that James had not stopped talking about me since that first conversation and that he was smitten (his words) with Julie. He also added that James was a nice lad, and I need not worry about phoning him."

"Wow. I had an admirer. A secret admirer nobody else knew, except his boss, and he wasn't likely to tell. The thing was, what should I do? There was no way I could see him, and did I really want to? In the end, my curiosity got the better of me and I went into Bakewell one Saturday morning, found a phone box, made sure nobody who knew me could see me, and phoned the number. James's Mum answered the phone and I asked if I could speak to James. She called him, put the phone down and I fought the urge to hang up and run away. Then James was saying hello and we had a good conversation and found out more about each other. He wasn't so shy on the phone and he said he liked talking to me. Also, he would phone me at the phone box next Saturday if I gave him the number, thereby saving me spending my pocket money. I looked forward to our Saturday conversations and began to think I might like to see him."

"I found out when we boarders were allowed to go to the cinema next and arranged for him to meet me inside - which seat, which row, which side, what time - and waited. We talked on the Saturday as usual and I was almost bursting with excitement, hugging my secret to me like a teddy bear. When the time came I went to the 'flics' with the usual suspects and I sat with them, as far away as I could find from the rendezvous seats. When the film started, I said I didn't feel too good and was going outside, in case I was sick. I crept to the other side of the cinema, heart banging like a drum, and there he was, exactly where we had planned. We sat and looked at each other, watched the film, held hands and whispered questions and answers. It was quite thrilling, but not in a romantic way, and I'm sure that it was the excitement of breaking rules and keeping secrets that fuelled my appetite."

"We arranged several more meetings, the last of which was in Derby during the May half term, to see Hard Day's Night with the Beatles starring. I was staying with my Gran and I told her that I was meeting Harriet, my school chum, and going to the pictures with her. She made sure I knew the bus times there and back and as I was almost 15, she trusted me to be safe."

"I realised after the film that James was not for me - after the first kiss and before the last coffee, and when I told him, he said he would never forget me, and I don't suppose he did."

Chapter 25

"Sunday mornings we all went to church - in our Sunday uniform, which for me was a pleated navy skirt and pale blue twinset. Boys wore a black jacket instead of a navy blazer. We went to the Anglican church, and I hated it. Stand up, sit down, chant, pray, shiver through the sermon behind a pillar so wide I could see nothing beyond it. Stand up, sing, kneel, pray, sing, go home. Two girl boarders — sisters - went to the Catholic church, and I was determined to go to the Methodist church, where the format was something I knew and felt comfortable with, and - if it was like Bethel Methodist church - would have warmth at its heart. My request was granted, mainly, I think, because several of the teachers at school were attenders and could report back if I should fail to turn up."

"Sunday afternoon was when the boarders were turfed out so that the boarding house staff could have some free time, and if it was wet we would be bussed up to Lady Manners school to use the gym, and whichever house master or mistress was on duty would supervise us. I liked the trampoline best, but it was popular, and I had to wait my turn."

"At one point later on, the girls' boarding housemistress was on long term sick leave with her first pregnancy and one of the PE teachers was standing in for her. She was great then, getting us playing games and having fun and exercise. But if she caught chatting after lights out or doing anything we shouldn't, we were dragged out of bed at 6 am and taken for a run on Mam Tor, which was boggy, misty and altogether no fun at all."

"I mostly avoided trouble."

"We were chatting quietly after lights out one night and we got onto the subject of favourite foods. Maxine mentioned chocolate, and before long we were drooling and groaning about the absence of any chocolate. Then I had a lightbulb moment. There was a machine in Bakewell marketplace that sold chocolate (and milk in cartons) for just sixpence. We weren't allowed out after dark and certainly not after lights out. *But.* I could get some Brownie points if I brought back the chocolate, so I offered."

"Silence. A couple of 'you shouldn't be taking a risk like that, Julie' comments and then, 'you wouldn't dare!' and that did it. Never say I daren't!"

"I waited till we could hear Miss Hopkins snoring next door, then I collected three sixpences from Maxine, Lydia and Lisa, crept downstairs, through the common room, down to the boot room where I put my coat on over my nightie, and my shoes, unbolted the door and out I went."

"Ten minutes later I was back with the goodies, the goodwill of my dorm mates who shared their bars with me, and a smug feeling of having won. I repeated this trip several times and somehow, never was caught out."

"You were a risk taker then, Julie?"

"Oh yes, Matthew, always up for adventure, that was me!"

"Our Sunday afternoon walks were very different, depending on who was accompanying us. Miss Hopkins preferred the riverside walks - to Haddon, Ashfield-in-the-Water, or Baslow - and we usually followed the same route in reverse coming back. Mr Hodges would march us up to Monsal Head or Great Longstone and return by a slightly different route."

"Mr Ritchie's walks were the best. We walked to Chatsworth via Edensor and back along the river through Baslow. We walked Froggatt Edge, Curbar Edge, Youlgreave, Tideswell, Bradley Dale, Monsal Dale, and more. We often arrived back late and supper had to be deferred, but the walks were always interesting, challenging and memorable. He would make sure that he walked beside every one of us, and chatted to us about ourselves, the history and geography of what we were seeing, generally making sure we were okay."

"At one point he asked me how I was faring in the bottom maths group. He had heard that I was doing very well in English and French, coming second in English and first in French in the exams. I told him that our maths teacher should be giving up teaching as she couldn't control the class, teach us much, or even notice when we were not there."

"He looked at me to see if I was serious. I was taking a bit of a liberty telling him this, and I smiled, to make it seem like a joke. He burst out laughing, telling me that similar comments had been floating round the staffroom, and then he stopped laughing and studied my face."

"He told me he had never seen me laugh or smile since I arrived, and that the effect was very encouraging. He said I wasn't to repeat what we had discussed, and that he would try to organise some extra tuition to get me through the maths GCE as he knew I had the intelligence to pass."

Chapter 26

"Halfway through the next week I was summoned by Mr Hodges, who told me that everyone was pleased at how well I was doing at school, and that my behaviour was improving. I was, he said, less 'prickly'."

"Mmm. Was that a good thing? People left you alone if you were 'prickly' and didn't expect too much. Anyway, he said, as my maths wasn't up to standard and the current situation in the bottom set was doing me no favours, Mr Ritchie had volunteered to give me extra tuition. On Mondays, Wednesdays and Fridays I was to do my homework as usual, but would begin at quarter to six, instead of six and go across to the boys' block at quarter to seven - or earlier, if I had completed all my other homework - and spend half an hour to three quarters of an hour going through the maths I'd need to know to pass my GCE in July. I should consider myself very fortunate to have been granted this favour and not waste the opportunity."

"A little bit of me was worried that I might actually not be up to the task. Another little bit of me felt a spark of something I didn't recognise, a hitherto absent sense of wonder that somebody wanted to do something to help me, and saw me as intelligent, worthwhile. My grandparents were the only people who had given me ... yes, a kind of loving ... from my earliest recollection. It was a weird feeling, and I kept wondering why. Why would someone like me deserve that kind of attention?"

"But I wasn't going to turn it down. No, I would throw myself into the mysteries of mathematics, the anathema of algebra, treat it like another foreign language (which it really and truly was to me)."

"So I presented myself at Mr Ritchie's door on Monday night at quarter to seven, and to my surprise, I was in his bedroom-cum-office-cum-lounge. It faced the girls' block with the pond in-between, so we were highly visible to the boarders doing homework in the dining room. They kept looking across for a week or so, then lost interest."

"We managed to get the basics of maths into my head. He was a very good teacher - I hadn't expected that, as he taught the top set, the brainy ones. When I made good progress and completed the exercises in good time, he would get a packet of biscuits from his desk and offer me one as a reward for working hard, and rather than send me back, we would chat about what we liked until the allotted time was up."

"It turned out that he was very much like my father in his ways, his cheerfulness, and like my dad was an only child and found it to be a curse as much as a blessing. We liked the same music, with the exception of jazz, which he liked - especially Dave Brubeck - and I loathed as it made me want to bang my head against the wall. He wasn't too keen on the Beach Boys' music, which I was passionate about. Classical music was something totally unfamiliar to me but he started playing it while we worked through the maths."

"Raif Vaughan Williams was the first composer who struck a chord - if you'll pardon the pun, Matthew - and we listened to his pastoral symphony, the Fantasia on a Theme by Thomas Tallis, A London Symphony, the Wasps, and many folk songs which soon became my favourite Classics. Then we moved on to Rimsky Korsakov, Scheherazade, until I began to see that there was a whole world of unexplored musical delight that I was on the verge of entering."

"We talked about many things - family, friends, art, politics, walking, although now I realise that I was naïve and lacking in real knowledge and understanding. I always came away from our sessions feeling buoyed up, and when Mr Ritchie said that I was very mature for my age, I was on top of the world. I found him to be quite different from the image I had previously held up as the Mr Ritchie who fools around with sixth formers."

"He told me about his family, where they lived and what they did, then asked about mine. I told him the whole story around six weeks into our tuition sessions. I didn't tell him about the doctor, or the reason I ran out of biology class. I didn't want his pity, and I didn't want him to know that I was a maladjusted, bad, dirty little girl who had been forced to grow up too soon. That was all put away in the darkest recesses of my mind, and from now on my life would be better."

"We became friends."

Chapter 27

"Life was looking good for me, Matthew. I was looked after, well fed, healthy. My hair had not been cut for two years, apart from a trim and a tidy up here and there. I weighed 8 stone 2lbs and was 5ft and half an inch tall. Doing well at school, even enjoying it."

"My Grandpa would drive himself, Granny and Dad up to see me when they could and I loved showing them Bakewell. I had a good friend at school, Harriet, and was lucky enough to be invited to her house half a dozen times, going home with her on the school bus to Grindleford and catching the public service bus back to Bakewell, which stopped right outside the boarding house. I was even getting invitations from parents who were school governors and wanted their sons and daughters to observe what a 'boarder' looked and behaved liked. I tried not to disappoint, and was interested to see how 'normal' families functioned."

"I was very jealous of Harriet. Her family was so full of love for each other. It was a house bathed in comfort and caring, although they were by no means well off. She had a brother and a sister older than herself, and three younger siblings. Two of them were twins, but not a bit alike. Laughter and cooking were always on the menu and her parents had a big garden and grew their own fruit and vegetables. The jealousy didn't last long as I knew our friendship would go a long way, and it has."

"I was in my final year at school, had been chosen to represent Glossop House in the spoken English competition, had been selected for the school hockey team, also for two events in the end of term sports day. I was in the school choir and was chosen to be a Gossip in Benjamin Britten's Noye's Fludde, performed on three evenings after school. So I had a lot to be happy about."

"Then I was summoned to Mr Hodge's office and told that my brother Michael had expressed a desire to see me."

"What? I hadn't seen him since I was seven and never gave him a thought, Early in our relationship I remembered him as being the reason nobody wanted to look after us when *she* was working. He had stood on one family's tortoise, another lady had a cat which didn't like Michael, and whenever he got an opportunity to kick it - or worse - he did just that. The crunch came when there was a dreadful yowling and he was discovered swinging the cat round by its tail. We were banished from every place *she* put us, he didn't like being anywhere other than by *her* side. Two of a kind."

"So what happened Julie, did you go to see him?"

"I had no choice, Matthew. I was put on a bus and met off the bus in Clay Cross, then taken to the institution where he had been for almost six years. It was awful. I hated every moment I was there. He – Michael - showed off the whole time and took every opportunity to make me look stupid."

"I stuck it out, though, counting the minutes to the time the bus would free me from this farce, and when I said goodbye to Michael I gave him the two finger salute. When he said he would see me again sometime I told him it would never happen, not if I had any control over the situation."

"Have you seen Michael since then?"

"No, Matthew. He got a girl pregnant, shot my dad's finger off, stole his motorbike and disappeared. He was last heard of in South Africa."

"That must have really hurt your mother, Julie?"

"Like I said, Matthew, they were two of a kind and deserved what they got. Anyway, *she* had another son, a houseful of lodgers, and no husband to get in her way."

"Hardly Happy Families, though, was it Julie. It has influenced your relationships with people, hasn't it?"

"It has made me a loner, self-reliant, independent, snatching affection from the very few people I can trust, and avoiding making friends who I am certain to lose. I'm very good at going it alone, never bored, and now I know what I am capable of. Which has taken time ..."

"Next time you can tell me if you got your maths O-level, and what became of Mr Ritchie. Till next week then, Julie."

Chapter 28

"Good morning, Julie, how are you?"

"I'm good Matthew, but I wasn't good when I got back to Castle Hill after seeing my brother - in fact I was seething. The homework hour had started and as I'd done my homework on the bus, I showed it to Mr Hodges and asked if I could go straight to my maths tuition, although I didn't really want to. The mood I was in was likely to get in the way of learning anything mathematical. But I went anyway, with my maths textbook, exercise book and rough jotter, which was meant for keeping notes, usually for copying up into the relevant subject exercise book."

"Mr Ritchie and I had developed a modus operandi over the six months' period or so. He would half-draw his curtain so that he was completely visible to anyone wanting to look, but I was sat in a chair to the right and not visible. We'd pass the exercise book between us as he wrote the theory, set me an example to work out and passed it back to me. It travelled back and forth as the tuition progressed and when it was over, the jotter would take its place and we conversed about many things. On this occasion, his first line was 'You don't look very happy, Julie.'"

"My reply – 'You don't look so jolly, either'.

'Do you want to tell me why?'

Pause: 'I had to go and see my brother in Clay Cross.'

'You obviously didn't enjoy that!'

'It was horrible. *He* is horrible. So what's the matter with *your* face?'

Pause: 'My girlfriend doesn't want to see me anymore. She says it's going nowhere and I seem distracted.'

'Well that's her loss, there are plenty more fish in the sea. Anyway, what does she mean by 'distracted'?'"

"He reached into a drawer in his desk and passed me his dictionary. I looked it up - *having one's thoughts or attention drawn away: unable to concentrate or give attention to something.*

"'Is she right, Mr Ritchie?'"

"As I pushed the jotter over to him and he reached to retrieve it, his hand touched mine. There was a tingle, like an electric shock that ran through me and made me hot, cold, uneasy, and yet I didn't want to move my hand away. He was looking at me with an indescribable look on his face, serious, yet like a little boy lost."

"I had to pull myself together and move my hand away, so I closed the jotter and put it with the exercise book. I asked him aloud, 'Are you distracted, Mr Ritchie? And if so, what is distracting you?'

'I am looking at my distraction, Julie. It's you.'

'But …, I …, you … I don't know what to say. I didn't mean to distract you.'

'Ever since I saw you on the Mound, howling like a creature in pain, all I have wanted was to make that pain go away, see you smile, be your friend …"

'And you are my friend, my true friend. You make everything bad go away …'

'But it has become something more.'

'Oh my God!'"

"The realisation dawned. Oh my God, what do I do? Where is this going? I stood up.

'I should go now, Mr Ritchie.'

'No, no sit down, Julie - we can't leave it like this. And for goodness' sake, my name is Brendon. When we are just the two of us you must call me Brendon. You are in shock, Julie, we need to sort out what happens next.'

'But it can't happen, Mr Ritch… - Brendon. You're a teacher and I'm a pupil. Anyway, how old are you?'

'I am 26, Julie, and you are 15. If you were a typical 15 year old, like most of the fifth form girls, I would not be falling in love with you.'"

"I nearly passed out. He had said it. The Love word. His face showed me that he was being honest. It was all too much. I burst into tears and sat back down in the chair with my face in my hands sobbing quietly, wondering how I was going to walk out of his room as if nothing had happened."

"After a minute or two he looked out of the window, saw, as I did, that the lights were off in the girls' block and he knelt down at my feet, took my hands gently from my face, pushed away some straggles of damp hair, then put both his hands round my face, tilting it up and holding it gently.

'Look at me, Julie,' he whispered. 'I have longed to do this, to touch your face, hold your hand, keep you safe and show you what love really means, but I can see that you are not ready to take it on board. I could try to forget you, move away, get a new job, I'd do anything I can to make you feel better, but what I really want to do is to wait until you are ready for us to be a couple, however long it takes. Please, Julie, please please don't push me away. I never felt this way about anybody before and it isn't wrong, not when two people feel the same way about each other. I'll wait as long as it takes. We belong together. Dry your eyes and we will see each other tomorrow, and talk about it some more."

"Oh my God Oh my God Oh my God. I didn't know whether to laugh, cry or howl at the moon. He offered me a clean handkerchief from his bedside chest of drawers and I wiped my face, blew my nose and gave it back to him. I wasn't sure about tomorrow, so I told Brendon I would think about it and perhaps see him the day after, for my next tuition session."

"I went straight to the dorm. The girls were listening to the Swinging Blue Jeans in the games room, so I got undressed and got into bed. When they came up I pretended to be asleep, so I heard Maxine say that it looked as if I'd been crying, and I had looked weird and a bit mad when I got back from my visit to my brother. If only they knew!"

"I spent that night with my mind in turmoil, my emotions on a rollercoaster, with the little girl inside me who was desperate to be loved telling me that the Beatles were right – love is all you need."

"I woke up to find Maxine standing over me looking concerned. She said she was sorry to have to wake me up but I was making a dreadful racket and it sounded like I was being murdered. I had been dreaming. My dad was lying on a river bed, a skeleton, and I was trying to get his bones out of the water, but they were coming away from the skeleton and I couldn't catch them before they were carried away by the current. I shuddered and told Maxine I was having a nightmare."

"She fetched me a sweet from her locker, kind soul that she was, and sat with me until I was quiet and had stopped shaking. I was afraid to go back to sleep in case I found myself back at the riverside, so I just kept turning over in my head all the possibilities on offer."

"I could ask Mr Ritchie – Brendon - to leave, go away, say we would forget each other."

"We could put everything on hold until after my O-levels, then look at the situation again."

"I could report him to Mr Hodges, the Headmaster, or someone in authority. He would be seen as an abuser."

"This was a chance for me to be loved and I could grab it with both hands and take the consequences."

"What was I to do? What would you have done in my place, Matthew?"

Chapter 29

"What would I do, you asked? I can't answer that, Julie, as I am not you. What would most people do? Again, everyone has a different story, a different set of values, different levels of nurture. I would very much like to know what you did do and why."

"Okay, Matthew. I did nothing. It was difficult, sitting in the dining room for breakfast and tea, knowing Brendon was sitting at the staff table and was directly facing me and my table. I could feel his eyes on me and imagine his anxiety. He had expressed his feelings in no uncertain terms and I was holding a live grenade in my hands. Take out the pin and BANG - everything goes up in the air and comes down in pieces. Destroyed."

"I had cried off the tuition session, feeling unwell. I looked unwell and I felt unwell. I didn't know how to face this situation. I was afraid, worried, curious, hopeful, and, for the first time ever, in a position to choose, to take control of my own life. This was the most terrifying thing to me and it should have been thrilling, exciting, the stuff of the great Classic novels. I tried to put myself in the place of D H Lawrence's heroines and found myself drawn to Cynthia, the Vicar's wife, who ran off with a penniless young man in his novel 'The Virgin and the Gypsy', not in terms of her circumstances, but in the emotional turbulence she was enduring."

"But this was *my* dilemma and I could not ask anyone to make the decision for me or help me to come to a decision."

"I couldn't avoid him forever, though, and the Christmas holiday was approaching. I didn't want to end the term on a bad note, so I asked Brendon if I could have a revision study time before the mock O-levels. He agreed and on the appointed day at the appointed time I knocked on his door."

"Walking into the room, the scenario from my last visit hit me in the face and I had to take a deep breath. Brendon looked very ill at ease and it was obvious that neither of us knew how to begin. We were polite, asking if the other was okay, then I sat in my chair, opened up my jotter and wrote in it -

Give me 10 reasons why you love me.

It came back:

1. *You are intelligent*
2. *You are sensitive*
3. *You need somebody (me) to love you*
4. *You are good to look at*

5. *You have a great sense of humour*
6. *I don't believe you would ever want to hurt me*
7. *You have got inside my head and my heart*
8. *I could never forget you*
9. *I can see us being together for a very long time*
10. *I want to turn your life around and make it joyful.*

I was impressed. I wrote again –

10 reasons why I should love you?

It came back –

1. *I really do love you*
2. *I can look after you properly*
3. *I am quite a nice kind of person*
4. *I am intelligent*
5. *I would never hurt you or ask you to do something you didn't want to do*
6. *My experience and maturity will keep you safe*
7. *I am not too ugly*
8. *I would help you to achieve any goals you have*
9. *My life would be too lonely without you*
10. *You will always be my best friend and my soulmate, regardless of what else you choose."*

"How did you remember this so well, Julie, or have you improvised?"

"I kept that jotter, Matthew. For years and

years. I must have read it a million times. Then I burnt it. But it is imprinted on my memory now."

"Ah, so did that resolve your dilemma?"

"What do you think Matthew? I will reveal all next week."

Chapter 30

"So, Matthew, are you ready for this?"

"I'm on tenterhooks Julie, tell all."

"Before I returned to the girls' block, Brendon had written his address and home telephone number in my jotter, with the instruction to write to him, phone him, or both. He said we should meet up in the holiday and see each other in a context that was more relaxed, with a view to getting to know each other better. I agreed, and wondered what I should tell my Gran. I didn't want to lie to her, but I couldn't imagine her being pleased about her only granddaughter dating a man - a man, not a boy - who was eleven years older."

"At the same time I wanted her opinion of him, needed her approval, and so I decided that I would give it some thought, away from Castle Hill, where it was beginning to overwhelm me."

"I managed to sit my mock GCE O-levels, only passing two of the seven, which rather surprised me as I had thought I would do better. Several teachers did say that the exams set as mocks were generally much harder than we could expect next June and we must not give up hope, but study hard and keep on target for the summer."

"My mind was on other things. I had started

to look in the mirror, something I had previously avoided doing as I didn't want to see myself as others saw me. I looked long and hard when there were no observers and tried to comprehend what Brendon had seen in me that had captivated him. I practised smiling, laughing, and what I hoped was being alluring, but all these faces seemed extremely silly to me."

"However, I took much more care in my appearance, buying egg and lemon shampoo and using a vinegar rinse to make my hair shine, and when I had washed my hair, I dried it with a hairdryer - a Christmas present - with my head down so that it had more volume, then I tied a ribbon round my neck over my hair, which made it turn up at the bottom and looked rather fetching, I thought. I also bought deodorant – the girls were quite impressed and included me now in their girlie chats. What would they have thought if they had known the reason I was making such efforts?"

"I had been seen talking to a lad, an 18 year old lad who had a motorbike. In the sixties, a lad with a motorbike would have the same status as a young man with a sports car today. His name was Graham and he was dating one of my classmates, Jenny Wolstenholme. Well, he was *supposed* to be dating her - he made it obvious that if I was interested in taking her place, he would most certainly ditch Jenny. I was loyal to my friends though, and just kept telling him that she was a much nicer person than me, and no matter how many times he stopped down the road from school and waited for me, I would never do more than chat to him. He was useful a couple of times, as you will hear later."

"So term ended and we all went home, or to relatives, for Christmas. When I got to the bungalow, Granny was in good spirits. Grandpa had had new windows put in on the front of the bungalow. They were bay windows with a wide curved sill inside where Granny had put her indoor plants - African violets and Streptocarpus, some ornaments and photos in frames. She had African violets in six different colours, all cuttings from friends. Among the collection of memorabilia was a framed copy of Stephen Grellet's often quoted statement -

But Once. I shall pass through this world but once. Any good therefore that I can do or any kindness that I can show to any human being, let me do it now. Let me not defer or neglect it for I shall not pass this way again.'"

"I must have looked at that framed mantra hundreds of times and knew it by heart. It was almost my role model for living. It summed up my grandmother to a tee and gave me focus for my life ..."

"Today, it spoke to me and told me that life was too short to deny it any chance of happiness. I was going to try this thing called romance that I had read so much about. Reading romantic novels had shown me that love was many different things to different women or girls, and there were so many aspects of love that did not sit well with my experience - or lack of experience - of love."

"It seemed inevitable that it would include looking into each other's eyes, holding hands, having fun, kissing, and then *sex*."

"No way could I in any shape or form consider repeating the act of brutalisation that had been inflicted on me by that dirty old paedophile and monster when I was nine. I had put it away and it only surfaced in nightmares, but it would be, for me, a reliving of that nightmare if I was expected to have sex with any man. What was I to do?"

"I spent hours in the library in Beeston, referencing every aspect of sex that I was capable of understanding."

"I went to see my dad in his shop, not so much to see *him*, but because I had made an appointment to see Dr Frost, as I was still registered at the Long Eaton surgery and I was looking forward to seeing him after more than two years away. He was pleased to see me and said I looked very well, that boarding school had done me a lot of good, it was clear. However, I explained that I had been carried out of assembly at school far too many times and told him about the heavy and erratic nature of my periods. He gave me a prescription for pills and asked me to make an appointment for six months' time, unless there were problems taking the medication. Great. I would be leaving school then."

"I knew that much because the Headmaster had interviewed me (along with all of the fifth year) and he had made it clear that, even if I were to achieve more than the two GCE's predicted, what he wanted for his 6th form was students with gumption (which I thought was furniture polish). And he suggested that I take a shorthand and typing course with a view to office work. Fine by me I thought, I just want to be a grownup, in a grownup world and have a proper boyfriend and a proper life, in which I made all of my own choices. I had become increasingly institutionalised, and it was bringing out the rebel in me once again."

"So, Julie, you were well along the road from adolescence to adulthood?"

"Mmm, so I thought, Matthew. So I thought."

Chapter 31

"Good afternoon, Matthew, I expect you are all agog to hear what happened next?"

"Good afternoon, Julie. Yes, but with some trepidation."

"Well, I was on cloud nine. I wandered round the peace garden in Beeston Memorial Square, aware for the first time of birdsong, Christmas roses, the bright lights and festive decorations in Beeston High Street and the smiles on peoples' faces. My world had been upgraded from sepia to a technicolour kaleidoscope of happiness. For the first time ever in my life I was in the driving seat, I had chosen and had been chosen to be loved. What a feeling, floating on a coral-bottomed lagoon by day, flying by night, high above the world, looking down on creation and being part of the beauty of the scenario below."

"I felt that the people I met saw me differently, as a person of integrity and value, and, best of all, I saw myself as someone who could achieve whatever I set out to do. The power of love has no bounds, love IS all you need."

"With a mixture of anticipation and fear I spent Christmas quietly until the time came for our rendezvous. Brendon and I met up on New

Year's Eve in Derby, but we walked around the city just talking, holding hands, stopping for a cup of coffee, stealing a kiss by the river where there were fewer observers. As it got dark, Brendon asked me if I liked steak. I had heard of steak, knew what it looked like, but its nearest relative that my Gran and I cooked was shin beef in a casserole, slowly braised in her aga. I said yes, I did like steak, then had a momentary panic when he asked did I prefer it rare, medium or well done. I hadn't a clue. I said rare hoping I sounded confident, and the corners of his mouth twitched in a little smile. Of course, he knew I was bluffing and would probably regret the choice, but then - and ever afterwards - he let me make my own mistakes and learn from them. He said he was taking me to a Berni Inn. I wondered what it would be like but didn't want to show my ignorance and ask."

"We set off and twenty minutes later arrived at Ramsden's Tavern in the Cornmarket, which had just been opened as a Berni Inn. So in we went, Brendon opening the door for me to go first. I was dumbfounded by the sight before me. Red Axminster carpets, white painted walls, subtle lighting, tables with gleaming cutlery and whiter than white napkins, table lamps made from wine bottles with a lit candle dripping wax down the green glass, and sparkling wine glasses."

"We were shown to a table in a corner and given menus. It was fairly easy, the starter was prawn cocktail or melon boat with Maraschino cherries, followed by steak, then Black Forest gateau or a cheeseboard, after which you could have Irish coffee and - extravagance indeed - an After Eight mint. I discovered that there were T-bone, sirloin, fillet and rump steaks, and in addition to rare medium and well done, I could order blue steak. Unable to imagine what had been done to the steak to make it blue, I stuck to my original choice of rare, and waited with anticipation to see what I had ordered. It is still my favourite way of eating steak, Matthew."

"Meanwhile, Brendon was scanning the wine list. I knew absolutely zilch about wine. The only wine I had even seen was the Crabbe's ginger wine that Granny drank on rare occasions instead of sherry. I had tasted some once when nobody was looking: it tasted 'interesting'."

"When the wine came, the waiter, with great showmanship and a folded napkin over his arm, uncorked the wine, poured a little of it into a wine glass and placed it in front of me with a flourish. I looked at Brendon, who had a mischievous look about him; he nodded and winked at me and I assumed that he wanted me to taste it for him. So I did. It was not something

I had done before, and the taste was strange but not unpleasant. The waiter then proceeded to fill two glasses then replace the bottle on the table. I asked Brendon what he thought he was doing. I was 15 – okay, 15 and a half, I should not be drinking wine. He said I didn't have to drink it, but I could do if I wanted to. He lowered his voice and leaned across the table and told me that he wanted to be the one who showed me new things, and introduced me to the world of grownups, where I belonged. But ... he smiled and put his hand over mine ... he was in no hurry, and we could take things as slowly as I needed them to be. So there was a dilemma."

There is a pause and Matthew is looking at his feet, his fingers interlocked and resting on his chest. After a full two minutes – I was looking at the clock - he looked at me.

"You do know what was going on here, don't you, Julie?"

"It has been pointed out to me that I was being 'groomed'."

"What's *your* view on that observation, Julie?"

"I refuse to see it that way, Matthew. It was the first time I had been truly loved and I didn't see the relationship as anything but natural, consensual and caring."

"But Julie, you were 15. You were still a child. He was abusing his position, as a teacher and as a responsible adult. He was dangerous."

"You didn't know him Matthew, you could never understand how he made me feel. I loved him."

Tears welled up in my eyes, making Matthew sit up, lean forward and put his hand on my arm.

"Don't cry Julie, I do understand. He gave you what you never had before, what you craved - love and attention. He made you feel special, showed you what your life could be like. What do you suppose he was getting out of your relationship?"

"Well, at the time I thought he was getting the same feelings as me. I was naïve, trusting and, I suppose, vulnerable."

"Which is why you were in a dilemma, Julie. You were presented with choices that you should not have had to deal with. You were still a child, and you had already had to deal with events that no child should ever have to deal with."

"I don't want to talk about it anymore, Matthew. I need to go home now."

"Okay Julie, but please promise me that if you get distressed about what we have discussed today, you will ring me and we can get you some help. Promise?"

He handed me his business card. I took it and left.

Chapter 32

"Hello Julie, how are you today?"

"I'm fine Matthew, but whatever you say about Brendon being a paedophile, it won't make any difference, I am just not prepared to accept that. So can we leave that subject right where it is and move on, please?"

"Of course. I was obliged to say what I said though. As your counsellor, I must point out what the rest of the world sees and makes sense of. Over to you now, Julie"

"I went back to Bakewell and tried to get on with living my life. It was so difficult, seeing Brendon every day and having to treat him like a teacher, avoiding eye contact, not even sneaking a look under my eyelids when I really wanted to run into his arms and feel his warmth, kiss him and feel safe and loved. Especially difficult were the Sundays when he took the boarders walking in Derbyshire. I had to wait my turn for conversation, act like I was just one of the boarders, and when he asked me if I had enjoyed the Christmas holiday I could have slapped his face!"

"So I said it could have been better, watching his expression change from self-assured to puzzlement, then a frown and the question – 'How could it have been better?' Just to annoy him I said that he wouldn't really want to know, and I dropped back into the group, starting a conversation up with Anne, the second eldest of the girl boarders."

"I felt mean, and kept asking myself why I had said what I did, and I had to conclude that I was being bitchy because I was jealous of anybody who spent time with Brendon when that was all I wanted to do. When we got back to Castle Hill he gave me a look which made me feel wretched. He looked hurt. I mouthed 'sorry' and went into the boot room hoping that nobody had noticed."

"Misery settled in and a black cloud of gloom chased away the sunshine of my days. The girls were asking me if I was okay as I didn't look well, and I used the time of the month excuse to ward off any further scrutiny."

"Towards the end of the first week back I had a letter brought to my table at breakfast. Each day, except Sundays, the boarders took it in turns to bring the mail and distribute it. As Dad and my Granny were the only people who wrote to me, I assumed it was from one or the other of them."

"I didn't recognise the handwriting, though, and was dreading the thought that it might be my brother, coerced into re-establishing the relationship we didn't have. When I opened it, it said very little, but it made me very relieved and joyful."

My dearest Juliet,

Amen, amen. But come what sorrow can,
It cannot countervail the exchange of joy
That one short minute gives me in her sight.

Forever yours,
Romeo'

"Was that not what Romeo said just before he and Juliet went to the priest to get married? Forever yours? Oh my God!"

"I'm nearly fainting with so many emotions chasing around inside me that I think I will surely die. Then I come to my senses and quickly stuff the letter and the envelope up my sleeve and do a quick recce to see if anyone has noticed anything. I had jokingly called him Romeo when we were kissing by the river in Derby, so the letter had to be from Brendon. He had cleverly adapted his writing, which was nothing like that in the maths book and my jotter, and which I now knew well. Had he forgiven me for my childish treatment of him, I wondered? It would seem so."

"I resisted the urge to look at him, smile, reply to his letter and speak to him, although I desperately wanted to do all of those things, but I did manage to put the smile back on my face and keep it there, and when our paths crossed at school (by my taking a different route to the science block) I gave him my best smile and received a beaming smile back."

"I got into learning mode now, it helped chase away the longing for the next break, half term, when we could be ourselves again."

"January passed in a flurry of revision, cold days and snow, making life as slippery as The Butts, the steep road which took us to Lady Manners. February started off cold but with blue skies most days. I was surprised again one morning to receive another letter, the handwriting the same as before. At least, I *thought* it was a letter, but it was in fact a card. A Valentine's card. Again from Romeo, but not attributable to Shakespeare. It said –"

My darling Juliet,

I spend all my time thinking of you and cannot wait until we meet again.

Forever yours,
Romeo'

"I was so absorbed in the feelings conveyed

that I didn't notice everyone on my table looking in my direction, and when Taffy snatched the card out of my hand, holding it out of my reach, I was horrified. Taffy (whose name was Evan Lloyd Hughes, and yes, he was Welsh) passed the card down the table to Daniel Duncan, who read it out while the rest of the table lapped it up and much hooting and commenting about 'Julie having a secret admirer' went on."

"Annoyed, I got up, walked round to Daniel and grabbed the card back. I felt an explanation was needed so I told everyone who was interested that they need not get excited as it was from Graham, Jenny Wolstenholme's boyfriend, with a motorbike, who kept pestering me for a date, and he didn't have a hope in hell of getting anything from me because I DIDN'T FANCY HIM!"

"It all went very quiet and I could see that all eyes were on me, including the top table where the staff sat. Brendon's face was a picture. Astonishment, fear, approval, all there on his face. Mr Hodges said could we all get on with our breakfasts and stop messing about and shouting. This was addressed to me, and I realised that I had indeed been shouting. I think I won that one though, as several boarders knew that Graham had a thing for me, the silly boy."

Chapter 33

"Hello Julie. We stopped last week at the point where you'd received a Valentine card. What happened next?"

"Hello Matthew. After school that day I went into the Library, not so much to change my books as to see if Brendon was there. He was. As I brushed past him I whispered 'anatomy', the section of the library furthest back and out of sight, and seconds later we were side by side seemingly absorbed in our selected books."

"'That was a close shave this morning,' Brendon said. 'You are enjoying living dangerously I suspect, my darling rascal. And who is Graham really?'

'He is who I said he was, Jenny Wolstenholme's boyfriend, who would like to be mine.'

'So, would you like him to be your boyfriend?'

'You must be kidding, he's just a boy. I only have eyes for you.'

'I hope so. But don't stop chatting to him, he's a useful cover. Speaking of which, we have to find a way of meeting up briefly just to connect. I feel miserable when I can't see you or talk to you for days at a time, and I really miss our tutoring sessions.'

'It would be too dangerous to be together in your room Brendon, I would have to kiss you ...'

'Stop it Julie, you're making me go weak at the knees just thinking about it. Think of a way we can meet up."'

"I thought about it, turning the pages of the book I wasn't reading, and came up with a plan. Between the end of tea and the beginning of homework, most of the girls would be in the games room, messing about or listening to records on the gramophone."

"I would go back to the dorm straight after tea on the pretext that I had left my homework, or part of it, there. Then I would close the curtains - which we always did when we were getting changed as our dorm faced the boys' block and Brendon's room - then open them again. That would be the signal for Brendon to come to the boot room. Nobody came into the boot room after 5pm, when the door was bolted. The access to it from the house was down six stairs, and if anyone were to come from that direction we would hear them well in advance and Brendon would have time to scoot out the door and away. We would try it out tonight."

"It worked a treat. We had 10 minutes together, exchanged our news, held each other close and kissed. It was exciting, thrilling, naughty. It kept us sane."

"When it was warm, we would meet up on the Mound. Curtains opened and closed twice. Easter was approaching and we talked about what we could do in the Easter holiday. Brendon said I must do lots of revision, as GCE exams would start at the end of May, and I nodded, in agreement."

"He had thought about us taking a whole day and walking, with a picnic lunch and a meal out afterwards. I could do revision on the bus and he would help me revise when we stopped for lunch. He had looked at suitable walks which we could do from Derby, where our buses would terminate, and had come up with Ambergate, which I knew as the bus from Beeston to Bakewell passed through it. It was mainly woods and a wide river. That thought got me through the rest of February and into March, and suddenly it was time to pack my bags and go back to Granny's."

"We had decided which day would be our day out, and I had all the details of bus times for the whole day. I told Granny that I was spending the day with Brendon, who was going to help me revise, and that I would need a packed lunch, and she was pleased that he was the sort of young man that had my interests at heart."

"The day came and it looked promising - blue sky, sunshine and warm for the time of year.

Granny had made egg and cress sandwiches with eggs from her hens - beautifully fresh with deep yellow yolks - and cress from the greenhouse, which was new and had replaced one of the two sheds which had finally collapsed."

"I had put on my favourite clothes, blue chambray Capri pants, cut off mid-calf, and a white cheesecloth top with embroidered smocking under the bust, sensible loafers for walking and a navy cord jacket which I had made with Granny's help."

"My bucket-shaped tartan bag had in it my sandwiches, a bottle of Lucozade, my purse, comb, revision books and the bus times for the day on a neatly folded piece of paper. I was ready in good time and caught the 9:15 am bus to Derby, arriving at 10:10. Brendon was waiting where my bus pulled in, and I resisted the urge to run into his arms, but my heart was tap dancing and I had the same feeling of it missing a beat that happened whenever I saw him. The bus for Ambergate pulled in 10 minutes later and we boarded it, grinning like children on a Sunday School outing."

"Twenty minutes later I remembered the revision, but we were so wrapped up in conversation, finding out more and more about each other, our lives, homes, family, dreams and hopes. Revision could wait."

Chapter 34

"When we stepped off the bus in Ambergate, it was a picture. The River Derwent was at its widest here and the skyline on all sides was forested slopes reaching towards the river. Brendon got out his Ordnance Survey map and pointed out the path we would take through the woods and the place we could stop. Off we went, happy in each other's company, holding hands, Brendon helping me over stiles and finding excuses to kiss my face, my neck, my nose, my freckles, and to loop my hair back over my ears, blow my fringe to one side, plait bits of hair, scoop it all up and pile it on top of my head. I tickled his back and wrote letters with my finger which he had to interpret and tell me the message I had written. I thought I would burst with happiness and wanted the feeling to last forever, and never end."

"After about two hours of walking, stopping, walking some more, Brendon taking photos, we stopped just off the footpath and down a grassy bank and Brendon dug deep into his rucksack, fetching out a fringed multicolour rug which he laid on the ground for us to sit on. We got out our sandwiches, I swapped one of my egg ones for one of his cheese and chutney sandwiches, and I was very pleased to find two slices of Granny's fruit cake wrapped in greaseproof paper. Brendon was pleased to eat one of them and shared his apple with me. After the food and drink, I got out my books and started to revise, but after half an hour, feeling a bit dozy, I put down the book and lay on my back, looking up through the leafy canopy, my eyes closing, Brendon squinting across at me, winking, putting his arm across my waist and then closing his eyes."

"When we woke up he checked his watch in alarm, but it was only half an hour later, still plenty of time for the bus. He took both my hands in his and looked deep into my eyes and told me that he wanted to wake up beside me every day for the rest of his life and he hoped I felt the same way."

"Of course I felt the same way!"

Chapter 35

"Looking at the map again we found a path downhill which was steeper and shorter and would avoid us missing the next bus back to Derby."

"We set off, but after 15 minutes realised that it was a much more difficult descent than we had anticipated. I had gone ahead and was looking back over my shoulder to make sure Brendon was okay, and I didn't see the tree root that tripped me up, making me fall sideways down the bank into a deep hollow full of dried autumn leaves and more tree roots."

"Brendon rushed over, his face full of concern, which relaxed when I started laughing. I felt silly, but we both laughed and laughed. Brendon held out his hand to pull me up out of the hollow. I grabbed it and pulled, but instead of him pulling me out, he lost his footing and fell into the hollow on top of me. More laughing and I was about to push him away when I felt an electric shock deep inside me and realised that the hardness pressing into my groin wasn't the penknife Brendon always carried in his pocket."

"The chemistry was impossible to resist, it was something bigger than both of us and we didn't *try* to resist it, pulling each other's clothes off and losing ourselves in the primitive instinctual passion that is sexual love."

"It was over in less than a minute, both of us stunned by the fierceness of the climax, but knowing that we were perfectly matched."

"A couple."

"I was surprised to find tears trickling down my face, and Brendon's face crumpled as he looked down at me. He told me he was sorry, he had not meant for this to happen, not yet, and he was so, so sorry he had made me cry. I interrupted him, saying these were tears of pure joy, he had made me happy and had nothing to be sorry for."

"The sun was setting, bathing us and the woods in its diffused glow of yellow, orange and red. The words Lawrence used to describe how Connie Chatterley felt came to mind."

'She was aware of a strange woman wakened up inside herself, a woman at once fierce and tender ... She felt herself full of wild, undirected power, that she wanted to let loose.'

"I felt loved and wanted."

Chapter 36

"Brendon gave me his handkerchief to mop up."

"We got dressed silently. I think we were both now a little embarrassed and very much stunned by the enormity of what we had done. I was ashamed that I had been so ready to willingly repeat an act of carnal depravity that was punishment for my badness. The fact that I had enjoyed every second of that brief moment of madness only confirmed that I was indeed no good, depraved, worthless, immoral and I would certainly go to Hell, and probably have to pay for my sins here on earth in the meantime."

"We walked in silence down onto the road and waited at the bus stop - silent, each of us unwilling to look the other in the eye, me because I didn't want to see rejection in his face, condemnation in his eyes. He was probably thinking of ways to finish with me, dirty little tart that I was. It hadn't taken him long to get what he wanted, after all."

"We sat on the bus, wordlessly looking out of the window, me to the left, Brendon to the right. I wanted to put my hand in his, look into his eyes, melt into a slow and gentle kiss, put my hand round his back, inside his jacket and pull him close to me, tell him I loved him and have him tell me that he loved me, too. It wasn't going to happen though."

"We walked through Derby silently, looking for somewhere to eat. It was almost dark now and the darkness made it easier to stop thinking. We ended up in an Italian restaurant which looked a bit shabby and where only four people were dining. Brendon led the way to a table as far away from the other diners as possible and we sat down. The waiter brought menus and we hid behind them. Brendon ordered chicken cacciatore for both of us and a bottle of wine which I was *not* going to protest about; I needed a glass of wine."

"Brendon looked at me, long and hard, and I waited, dreading what I knew was coming. He said:

'Julie, my darling Julie. It wasn't meant to happen this way. I couldn't control my feelings for you. You have taken over my heart, my mind, my body in a way that nobody has ever done before. I love you.'"

"I must have been gawping at him in disbelief. My throat was dry, my heart beating like a drum, my mouth open. I felt faint, hot then cold. He leaned over and put his hand on my arm and I pulled myself together."

"'You look very pale, Julie. Are you alright?'
'I thought you were going to finish with

me,' I whispered.

'Why would I want to do that? I wasn't going to rush anything, but I can see us being together, even married. But you are not sixteen yet and I should not have made love to you, and you should not have let me.'

'I feel the same way Brendon, I couldn't help myself. What are we going to do?'

'We must make sure that it doesn't happen again, Julie. Where are you with your menstrual cycle?'

'What? Do you mean …' I lowered my voice … 'my periods?'

'Yes, when are you next due?'

'I'm not sure. In a week or more, I think. Why?'

'I might have got you pregnant.' It hadn't occurred to me until then, but yes, it was a possibility.

'And if you have, what then?'

'I will do whatever you want me to do, but I have to say that it wouldn't be a good outcome for either of us."'

"My mind in an act of treachery took me back to the nine year old child who was raped without even knowing what was being done to her by an old man with a very thin penis, and revulsion spread through my body, threatening to make me vomit before I had even tasted the food. But in no way could I relate that experience to what Brendon and I had shared. It was utterly and completely different. And Brendon loved me. And I loved Brendon. But he must never ever know about the nine year old Julie."

"I told him that I would think about what we should do and I told him that I loved him, regardless of what was to be. We enjoyed the meal and the wine, Chianti it said on the label. We walked to the bus station and just held each other. When my bus came in he kissed me briefly but firmly and said he would phone me at my Gran's tomorrow."

"Wow! That is intensely emotional, Julie. A real love story."

"My feelings were all over the place Matthew, but I couldn't help feeling that it was the best love story ever."

"And I was the heroine for the first time ever."

Chapter 37

"When I got home to Gran's it was late, but she was waiting up for me. Gramps had gone to bed. She scrutinised me until I asked what was the matter and she said she had been worried about me. Feeling a hot flush envelop my face I half turned towards my bedroom, telling her that she need not worry about me as I was quite capable of looking after myself."

"Was I? It seems not. I had discovered feelings that I could not handle, alien, but mad, passionate, out of control, delicious, rapturous feelings, never conceived of in any shape or form, awake or dreaming. Yes, it even beat my flying dreams!"

"'You're not getting in too deep with this Brendon fellow are you, Julie?'

'Why do you ask me that?' I replied.

'You have a look about you,' she said. 'I know that look and it worries me. You're not sixteen yet, still have exams to do and school to finish. And then we need to talk about what you will do in July when you finish school. Whether you go back as a sixth former or get a job.'

'Can we talk about it tomorrow? I'm really tired.' I turned to face Granny. 'Please don't worry about me, I will be fine and dandy.'"

"She smiled. 'I only hope so. Goodnight

love, sleep tight.'

'Mind the bedbugs don't bite!' I smiled back."

"I got ready for bed, looking at myself in the oval mirror above the fireplace. I rarely looked in the mirror, and then only to check that my centre parting was straight, but I put my face close up to it to see if I looked any different. This 'look about me' was invisible to my eyes, but I certainly felt different, like Alvina, D H Lawrence's lost girl, who rejects family, society and its expectations and goes out to pursue a life where she can exercise her high-spirited aims with her strong will, making her admired by some and despised by most. Like Alvina, I felt ahead of my time, a woman in a girl's body. I looked at my body in the mirror, it was boyish, with my small breasts and narrow hips, flat stomach and rounded buttocks, and I could see no beauty in it, but when I thought about Brendon, on top of me, inside me, I felt a hot flame of desire, a need for the flesh of his body to be inseparable from my flesh, which made my knees feel weak and my heart beat fast. Oh God. How could I stop this feeling? Did I want to? No. I prayed that night that God would take me and change me and tomorrow I would wake up as somebody else."

"My dreams were full of challenging

situations, needing decisions to be made, deception and lies, my Gran was trying to protect me from wild animals whose teeth dripped with blood. I couldn't run, my feet were stuck in shifting sand, the beasts were turning round to eat Granny. There was a cliff top, nowhere to run to, the baby I was trying to save from them dropped out of my arms, the beasts were driving me to the edge, I screamed as I went over it ..."

"I woke up to see Granny with a cup of tea, telling me I had been making the strangest noises in my sleep, as if I was being murdered. Was I alright?"

"'Just a bad dream,' I grinned. 'I am glad to be awake after that dream.'"

"She went back to the kitchen and I pondered for a moment, drinking my tea. I was still the same me, No God, then. I would have to fight all my own battles, make my own decisions, find my own place in the world. What if I was pregnant? I decided to make an appointment with Dr Frost and talk about avoiding being pregnant again."

"I spent the morning talking over my options about school, telling Granny that the headmaster at Lady Manners had little hope of me gaining the exam results which would take me to the 6th form and that I was more inclined to look for work."

"As the Chairman of Beeston and Stapleford District Council Granny was often invited to inspect local businesses, and she had recently visited The Boots Pure Drug Company in Beeston. She was impressed with their work ethic. Anyone who started with them aged sixteen would benefit from a day a week in their own college of further education, and all employees received shares in the company as part of their wages."

"The salary structure was good, and it would be within cycling distance. The bike one of my dad's cousin's children had donated to me was in the garage and Gramps could soon fix it up to be fit to ride. I was welcome to stay with them for as long as I wanted, but there were plenty of flats and bedsitters I could look at once I had saved enough to put down a deposit."

"I said it all sounded good, and I looked up the phone number in the telephone directory, rang the Boots Personnel department and arranged an interview. Then I phoned the surgery in Long Eaton to see the Doctor."

"Brendon phoned just before lunch and I told him the news. He was concerned about how I felt and said he hadn't slept well last night. I told him about my dreams, the interview in two days, and asked when we could see each other again. He said we should wait until we knew that

I was 'okay', and though disappointed, I knew it was advisable, especially as my Gran was worried that I was getting too involved. There was a long silence when I told him that, and I held my breath. He surprised me by saying it was time he met my Gran."

Chapter 38

"Well, Julie, I'm wondering how the meeting went and if Brendon impressed your Grandma?"

"I was excited, Matthew. I desperately needed my Gran's approval of the man I had fallen in love with. I knew that once she had met him there would be no worries about him being older than me, but at the same time it wouldn't be wise to let her know how far the relationship had progressed, and she was intuitive enough to put two and two together and make four!"

"I said I would talk to her about it and ring him back that evening. Brendon's parents were quite old - he was a late arrival when his Mum was nearly forty, so they were around the same age as my grandparents. So Brendon was used to having older people to deal with - even, I discovered, very good at it."

"Granny was tickled pink that he wanted to meet her and Grandpa and immediately said I should invite him for lunch on Friday as I would be going back to Bakewell on the Saturday."

"I had noticed amongst the mail that morning a letter to Gran with handwriting that was familiar, and asked if it was from *her*. She frowned and said it was indeed from my mother, the latest in a long line of abusive letters, many of which she had burned. My dad had recently asked her to keep them as they might prove useful in his defence when the divorce proceedings went ahead."

"I asked if I could see the letter, and Granny said that as I was almost sixteen and I was mentioned in the letter, I probably had a right to see it. I told her that nothing *she* could say or write would change any opinion I had of my Granny or of *her*. I read the letter and even though I knew what nastiness she was capable of, I was shocked at the vitriol it spat out at me. This is the letter, Matthew."

'Mrs B

Your influence is the sole cause of all my marital troubles and the main reason Julie left home. I will ensure that you will NEVER see my boys again if you continue to stir up more trouble and you are NOT going to break up what bit of the family that loves each other and desires to stay together.

I intend to find another father for my boys and it will depend on YOUR behaviour as to how near or far from their original father they will eventually live. You, John and Julie are all made in the same mould and you all think yourselves better than everybody else and cleverer than everybody else, but you are NOT.

You have interfered from the start of our marriage, giving advice and gifts of furniture which were both unwanted and unasked for and you have encouraged all the bad behaviour and eating problems Julie has had by spoiling her with the intention of making her like you and despise me. Just mind your own business and leave me to mind mine.

Mrs B. Junior.'

"Wow! She certainly didn't hold back, did she?"

"No, Matthew. I asked if I could look at some more of the letters, and you can't imagine hate-mail like it. She blamed my Gran for all that was wrong with *her* and claimed that Granny had poisoned people against her by making up and spreading lies to all her friends and neighbours. I asked Granny what *she* meant by this, and I learned that, far from causing trouble, my grandma had, on several occasions, prevented her from being in trouble with the Authorities. When she'd been caught shoplifting and was facing prison, for instance, Granny used her influence as a Justice of the Peace to keep my mother out of prison on the grounds that she was suffering from postnatal depression, organising instead that she return to her parents' home for six

199

months with her son."

"That was why my dad was on his own when he came to Woodhouse Eaves to see me."

"I learned also that among her political friends at County Hall was Mrs Brown, who lived across the road from our house at Cowley Street, Basford. It was Mrs Brown who told Gran about the coming demolition order and suggested that the house could be bought for less than its market value and would make an ideal home for newly-weds for 10 years. And yes, it was Mrs Brown who kept an eye on me (and on *her*) and had telephoned to report to Granny any issues that she felt were not good parenting."

"So yes, she did interfere. Granny had begged my mother to let me go and live with her in Beeston. That was the ultimate insult and also the trump card for *her*. No way would *she* ever agree to that, even though she reiterated many times in her letters that I was badly behaved, didn't respond to tellings-off and punishment and that I got on her nerves to the point where she wanted me out of her sight. I will bring the letters I have kept next week, Matthew, and you can get a flavour of our family life."

"Mmm, I'm not sure I look forward to reading them Julie, but it's good to get another perspective. See you next week then. Bye."

Chapter 39

"Hello Matthew, I'm sorry I had to cancel last week's session, but I had a chest infection and lost my voice."

"I hope you are feeling better now Julie. Thank you for sending me the letters. I have had time to read them. Here they are."

Matthew passed the letters to me in the big manilla envelope I had posted them in. "They don't make comfortable reading, and I suggest you don't make a habit of going through them."

"Several themes jump out of them which I would like to discuss today, Matthew, and then I'll leave them behind in the past where they belong."

"What did you find was a recurrent theme, Julie?"

"The main theme was that *she* was jealous of my Gran, although she disguises it as resentment."

"Well spotted Julie. She cannot bear the fact that your father's mother still came first, and everybody and everything else came second, or worse, had no interest to him."

"He disappointed *her*, Matthew. He was a spoilt only child, not as clever as *she* expected him to be and he had no interest in his children. He relied heavily on his Mum and was disinclined to discipline me and my brothers."

"Was he really a spoilt child?"

"Only in the sense that he didn't have to share with siblings his parents time and love, possessions and attention. He found it difficult to find work when he was decommissioned from the RAF after World War 2, so not only was he unable to provide a steady income, but his self-esteem rapidly dropped through the floor. It must have made him anxious. No wonder he was not the best father."

"That brings me nicely to another recurrent theme. What do you think that might be?"

"Attention, Matthew. *She* was forever saying that I was attention-seeking. Well of course I was! I was never going to win their affection, so I grabbed the only attention available by being naughty. I was well aware that I was being rude, poking around in places I shouldn't, taking things that didn't belong to me and doing silly things, like putting my finger in the door frame and closing the door - risking trapping my finger - just for the effect it would cause."

"I used to dream that I was dying. It was great because everybody came to watch me die and they all felt guilty because they were the cause of my death, and that was enough to satisfy my needs."

"That's very tragic, Julie. Did you ever see your mother again?"

"I saw her once, Matthew, on the day of my dad's funeral. She didn't go to the service, but I knew she would be back at Canal Street afterwards, raking through Dad's stuff, burning it. I asked her if she had come to dance on his coffin. Those were the last words I spoke to her. I was 33 at the time."

"You are amazing, Julie. A survivor. No, don't cry, you didn't get this far by feeling sorry for yourself. Far from it. You used the negative influence to make you able to fill your life with only positive actions and thoughts."

"Most of the time, yes, but there were times ahead when it all fell apart, and that's another story."

"Back to the letters then. What else do you suppose I found recurring in them?"

"My guess is the fact that *she* was criticised, directly and indirectly, for being a failure as a wife and mother by my Gran, and because it was a valid criticism, she resented it hugely and hated my Gran for trying to help and give advice. And so *she* was forever demanding an apology, making that the stumbling block in the relations between her and her in-laws."

"What's your view on that?"

"*She* operated best in an office, Matthew.

She was articulate, a good typist and in her element in a business environment. She knew she wasn't cut out to be a mother, and it must have been very difficult for her. She mentions several times that she was on the edge of a nervous breakdown, and that she wanted to be as far away from me as possible."

"She may have suffered post–natal depression, Julie. In those days it wasn't recognised or treated."

"Maybe. I know how demanding children can be. There was a nasty streak in *her* though, which was inherent. Her own upbringing was far from perfect - her younger sister was the bright light in the family and *she* was always second best. So nature and nurture conspired to make her what she was."

"That's a very balanced view. Your own experiences have obviously tempered your attitude to parenting."

"The only thing I cannot forgive her, Matthew, is that she never tried to make life better for her own children than hers had been. I was determined to end that cycle of abuse when I had my own children and largely, I succeeded, thank God."

"Is there anything else you want to talk about regarding the letters, Julie, before we consign them to the archive?"

"I have to say Matthew, that my Gran may have seemed like she was persecuting *her* for her shortcomings, but she did it out of love for her son and her granddaughter, and I can never hold that against her. Indeed, I might not be alive to tell the tale had she not intervened."

"But you are alive, and you seem to have put it all into perspective, Julie. Next week I look forward to hearing about Brendon coming to meet Granny!"

Chapter 40

"Hello, Julie, I'm really looking forward to hearing about the introduction."

"Morning Matthew, here we go then. I phoned Brendon back to invite him for lunch on Friday. I was nervous, excited, unsure and resolved, in equal measures. Also, until tomorrow I would not know whether I was pregnant."

"It had never been part of my plan to have a baby. I was not ready for that kind of responsibility or the damper it would cast on my life. At the same time, I was so in love with Brendon that I would have done anything to keep him, and might even have found it enjoyable. The jury was out on that one, and all I really wanted was to have him close to me and revel in the new intimacy we had accidentally created, although that was hardly appropriate for the meeting with my family, such as it was."

"Brendon was pleased to be invited and accepted without demur."

"He asked how I was feeling and I said I was fine, just impatient to see him again. He reminded me that what happened in the woods was not planned but that he felt even more strongly that we had something very special, and he said that he could hardly wait to see me and hold me close again."

"Also, if I was pregnant we would get married a.s.a.p. What!?"

"I felt that melting feeling again, and it was a factor in our love that every time I saw him or thought about him that feeling remained throughout our relationship, a physical desire that resurged again and again with never relenting force."

"But … I had to maintain a status quo when we were not alone, and I had to start now. I brought the conversation back to trivial concerns and told Brendon that I would be seeing Dr Frost the next day after my interview at Boots, and he wished me luck in both events."

"The interview went very well, I thought. They seemed to ask me the right questions and I think I gave the right answers. I gave them a more positive picture of my expected exam results than reality suggested and was very interested in the day at Boots College offered along with the position. All in all I think we were all very pleased with the interview and I was told that the job offer would arrive in the post if I was successful."

"I felt optimistic, and decided that for a first interview it had gone well, but I wasn't going to count my chickens until they hatched."

"The doctor's appointment provided several surprises. His first question to me was had I been taking the pills regularly as prescribed? Yes, I had. Were my periods more regular and less painful? Yes, they were. Third question, was I in a sexual relationship with my boyfriend?"

"I blushed a deep red, feeling the heat rise from my throat upwards. Before I could get back to a position where I could answer that, Dr Frost smiled and said that it was written all over my face and body that somebody loved me and that I felt the same way. He was right of course, and I began to worry that if it was obvious to him then the whole world would read my body language and I would never be in control again."

"The doctor reassured me that it was part of his calling to see beyond the outward presentation of his patients. I need not worry, he said, as our conversations were only between the two of us and not open to anyone else. He asked again if we had crossed the line and become intimate, and I told the story of our first sexual experience. I said that I was a bit worried as we had not taken any precautions and was taken aback when he laughed - a great guffaw that I was puzzled to find a reason for. When he got control of himself he explained that the pills I was taking were contraceptive pills, which had the secondary effect of regulating the menstrual cycle, so effectively I was covered against becoming pregnant. Not experiencing the blackouts and heavy bleeding that had previously darkened my days was the bonus. I was gobsmacked!"

"Dr Frost examined me anyway and said that I was in good shape, had a whole new world to look forward to exploring, and he hoped that my boyfriend appreciated how lucky he was. He gave me another prescription, winking conspiratorially at me as he handed it to me."

"Wow. My kneejerk reaction was to phone Brendon right away from a phone box, but I resisted the temptation and went to see my dad, feeling rather smug. Dad was in one of his dismal moods, He tended to think that it only rained on the side of the street where he walked and his glass was always half empty, so I came away feeling a little depressed, but the bus journey back to Beeston restored the euphoria and I got back to Gran's just as the phone was ringing."

"It was Brendon, and I told him that all had gone well. I was hopeful of good outcomes all round and I would explain tomorrow. We looked forward to being together again and for once, I went to sleep that night in a happy state and found myself flying in my dreams over a peaceful landscape, full of beautiful flora and fauna and with the sounds of Vaughan Williams' Pastoral suite lulling me into a deep sense of contentment."

"The next day Gran and I prepared lunch after the breakfast and housework rituals had been performed, and, keen to make a good impression, Gran got out and washed her best cutlery and crockery. We collected the braising steak from the butcher's. Gran had no fridge or freezer, so meat was bought daily and kept in a green painted metal meat safe with ventilation holes in the sides, allowing air, but not flies, to access the contents."

"She had a marble slab in what had been my dad's bedroom and was now a glory hole (her words) for whatever didn't fit or belong in any other room. It was always a joy in my younger days to explore the mysteries this room presented and Granny never minded what I unearthed, in fact she had stories about everything stored in there and was happy to tell me those tales. Nowadays she would tell the same stories, but sometimes there was a new detail or a twist in the story that made me always listen carefully, even though I knew most of the stories by heart. Today, as we were putting together a rhubarb and apple crumble for pudding, she reminded me of the time, after she and William got married, that she moved into her mother-in-law's house."

"Gran's family had decided at the outbreak of war that they would leave Nottingham, which was considered at risk, and move to Coventry, where several relatives lived already. I don't need to say that they came to regret this move, but as Gran had just married Will, her fiancé, she had no urge to go with her family to Coventry. They lived with his parents until the bungalow was built and Rhoda, her mother-in-law, taught my Gran as much as she could about cooking and keeping the house in a good state. Whenever they got chatting and forgetting that the oven was full of cakes, biscuits or pastries, Rhoda would dash to the oven, waft away the smoke that came out with the blackened contents and my Gran would say, 'never mind, they'll do for our Bill.' At which point they would collapse in a fit of giggles before starting again."

"Everything was ready and I went to set the table in the front living room. Looking up, I saw Brendon opening the gate, threw the cutlery on the table and rushed out, saying I would show Brendon the garden before bringing him inside. Granny smiled her 'I know what you are about, young lady' smile and out I ran. I garbled the news that Dr Frost had given me, briefly covered the interview, then dutifully gave him a tour of the garden, sneaking a kiss under the plum tree which was out of sight of the kitchen window."

"We went inside and Brendon shook hands with Gran. She wasn't having any of that!"

"'Come here young man and let me give

you a hug. That's the least you deserve if you're going to be part of the family!'"

"She gave him a good looking over and said, 'well, I suppose you'll do, and our Julie obviously thinks you will.'"

"We laughed, and the ice was broken. Brendon was genuinely interested in what she did, and when Gramps came home from work for his lunch, I might as well not have been there. The conversation and ambience were very jolly and I found myself a spectator rather than a participator, but I didn't mind one bit. It was evident that they were both going to get on with my choice of partner."

Chapter 41

"Brendon had brought chocolates for Granny and the newly released 'Pet Sounds' LP by the Beach Boys for me, so after lunch we left Granny eating chocolates in the front room while we washed up. Then we walked down the road to the river. I pointed out Gran's neighbour's boat and we chatted in depth about the job interview and the news from Dr Frost. It was of course a great relief to us both. We planned to keep sex off the menu till after the O-Level exams and my sixteenth birthday. Then we went back to Gran's and played my new LP on the record player Brendon had given me for Christmas, along with Scheherezade, a classical music composition by Rimsky Korsakov."

"Granny popped her head round the door to say there was a cup of tea made and that they - nodding her head at the record player - sounded like a bunch of choirboys! They did, actually, but I never stopped loving their songs."

"All too soon it was time for Brendon to go and get his bus back to Sutton-in–Ashfield."

"I packed my suitcase later that evening ready to go back to Bakewell. Of course, I had to ask Granny what she really thought about Brendon. She thought he was genuine, caring, reliable, all the things that made a man worth his salt, (her words) and as I had an old head on young shoulders, I shouldn't mind about the age gap at this stage. She added that the age difference would be more of a challenge when Brendon reached middle age. Naturally, I wasn't going to even think that far ahead. 'Just enjoy it while it lasts,' was her advice, 'and don't go getting up to anything you might regret, young lady!' was her warning."

"Back at Castle Hill it seemed different, as if the place had shrunk. Maybe it was because I was beginning to think of it as somewhere I was about to leave, to go out into the big wide world beyond its confines, physical and psychological. I don't know. There was a growing impatience within me that nothing seemed to chase away, a need to cast off the chains of childhood and see myself as a young woman. Granny had addressed me as 'young lady', so she must have seen that I was developing a persona more in keeping with an adult."

"I told Brendon this when we managed one of our trysts on the mound and he looked me in the eye for what seemed like a lifetime and said that he had witnessed the same change in me, too. I wondered if it was beginning a sexual relationship that was the cause. Brendon considered this silently for a while, then he turned to me and there were tears in his eyes."

"Shocked, I asked why, and he said he would not have stolen my childhood from me if he had had the self—control to hold back. Now I was crying too, and I managed to splutter out that it was me that encouraged him and neither of us was to blame."

"My childhood was not stolen, I reassured Brendon, it was transformed into a state of being loved, unlike anything I had ever known. We held each other tight and I really didn't want to ever let him go. The bell was ringing for tea, though, so we parted with an aching that seemed impossible for me to bear."

"The Ambergate scenario kept running in my head and the physicality of the reaction was mind blowing. It felt like I was being taken over by a carnal force of pure passion and desire, and it stopped me from getting on with the day to day business of learning, revising, communicating and eating. My co—boarders probably thought I was suffering from exam nerves, and they tried to encourage me to join in with their madness, dancing and miming to The Rolling Stones, The Animals, The Righteous Brothers, Unchained Melody ...'Woah my love, my darlin', I hunger for your touch' ... Oh my God, how I hungered for Brendon's touch! I was going mad, my emotions tossing around like a line full of washing on a windy day."

"When we grabbed our daily ten minutes before tea we kissed solidly for the whole ten minutes, hardly surfacing for breath, and I knew that he wanted me as much as I wanted him. My birthday was just weeks away and the idea of waiting was out of the window."

"Then came a lucky break. In two weeks' time there would be a Boarders weekend, when we all went home on Friday and came back on Sunday. These weekends usually happened when the staff needed a break or were away on business or on holiday, but the reason this time was that The Hodges were called away to look after a relative coming out of hospital. Also, they said, it would give year 5 a chance to revise away from the distractions of boarding life. However, when my Gran was informed, she said it wasn't possible for me to stay with her as she and Gramps were going away that weekend to a Conference at which my Granny was speaking. No way would I go to Long Eaton - everyone was aware that my parents were divorcing. So I would have to stay at Castle Hill on my own."

"I acted upset and could have won an Oscar for my performance, while inside I was leaping and shouting for joy. The possibilities that this opened up kept me sane for the two weeks, and I was very busy planning trysts and romantic rendezvous and not at all busy revising."

"The Friday came, and by 7 pm the only person at Castle Hill was me. Brendon had 'disappeared' - ostensibly to catch a bus home. He reappeared at 10 pm but didn't put his light on. The room in our block next to the bathroom had been Anne's room but had been empty since the end of May when she'd returned to Singapore. In it was the building's only fire escape, with steps down to the top of the mound, then twelve steps down from the mound to the ground."

"I was waiting in Anne's room and when I heard Brendon on the steps outside, I opened the door to the fire escape."

"I don't want to go into detail and make it sound like a Barbara Cartland romance. Let's just say that the experience was a voyage of discovery. We took our time, taking in the way our bodies looked, touching and loving the feel of skin on skin, making love as it should be made, each desiring to please and each reaching our climax together in an earth shattering blast of exquisite fusion. It was almost pain. The most incredible union two people can experience. I have to say I have never experienced that same feeling with anyone else, but then I have never been so in love with anyone else. Probably my fault."

"Julie, that sounds amazing the way you

describe it. But first love is often built up to be special afterwards because we feel the need to tag it as a milestone. Could that be the case here?"

"Oh no Matthew, this *was* special. It was real love, not just a first teenage romance."

Matthew pursed his lips and frowned. "It was also very dangerous."

Chapter 42

"Dangerous, you said last week Matthew. We both knew it was dangerous, for so many reasons. But reason was out of the window and the danger also gave the thrill a razor–like edge that was intoxicating."

"I didn't care. I only cared about keeping this man I loved so deeply. The rest of life didn't matter. Brendon had the most to lose. His reputation, his job, maybe even his career, and that should have made me care. I was still a teenager, but my emotional maturity was so underdeveloped that I didn't have the means to think beyond the present. I could only dream of the future, in the same way that I'd dreamed of having a party when I was five years old."

"That's a valid point Julie. It's only through experience that we gain wisdom, and you had had precious little experience of love as a child."

"Well, I was determined not to miss out from that moment onwards. My poor mind was going round in circles which began and ended with Brendon and how he made me feel. Every touch, every inch of him, was uppermost in my thoughts and I was totally under the spell of his capacity to make me feel special. Years later, when I read 'Madame Bovary' by Gustav Flaubert, I understood completely how Rodolfo was - to Emma - an escape from the monotonous trivia her life had become - so much so that she risked her husband and baby waking up and catching her out as she indulged in her romantic and sexually fulfilling midnight rendezvous at the bottom of her garden. I am relieved that my life turned out better than hers, though, as she poisoned herself in a most horrible ending to her unfulfilled life."

"Brendon and I had another night which we could spend together, and I was on tenterhooks imagining how it would go. I had my meals for the two days in the fridge in the kitchen, but threw most of it in the bin, as my mind was far away from eating. Instead I binged on crisps and chocolate wafer biscuits foraged from the store cupboard, along with apples from the tree on the mound. I suggested that Brendon and I could meet up in the daytime, but he said that would be unwise, so I settled down to revise."

"Instead, I devised an alternative way to spend a night together which would work when the boarders and staff were all back in residence."

"Next to Anne's empty room was the bathroom. There was always a top window in there left open (for obvious reasons), and if I was able to climb out of that window and stand on the ledge, it was only a two foot step across to the fire escape rail. If Brendon left his bathroom window open, I could run across, keeping close to the wall, turn right at the pond and climb into his bathroom. Then, if I made sure the boot room was unbolted when I went to bed, it was a fairly easy task to get from the boot room to the floor below ours, then up to my floor and back to bed. I discussed this with Brendon when we met on the mound and he was against the idea at first, pointing out that it was a twenty-five-foot drop to the ground from that bathroom window. I said that it would mean we could spend more time together, and that tonight we could even spend the whole night in his bed."

"In the end he gave in and although he would, he said, be anxious until I reached him, he couldn't resist the temptation of another night of passion."

"Almost delirious with expectation, I calmed myself down by soaking in a long bath with added bubbles 'borrowed' from Maxine. We girls used to share stuff on a regular basis, so it wasn't stealing."

"I washed my hair and gave it the works - shampooed twice, rinsed with vinegar to make it shine, blow dried to a damp stage then curling the ends around a brush, blow drying on a low heat to avoid splitting the ends - and I felt very satisfied with the outcome. I stood naked in front of the full length landing mirror, something I had never done before and would certainly never do again. My shape had changed in the last six months and become less boyish, with rounded but not big breasts, a very narrow waist and hips that were evident but not wide. My bottom was my best feature, being round but firm and smooth. I had a long back but short arms and legs, which annoyed me from that day to this, as sleeves were always too long unless three quarter length and trousers always too long - until Capri pants became fashionable I always had to cut eight to ten inches off the legs!"

"I listened to Lydia's radio - Radio Caroline playing pop music 24/7 - and I sang along to the songs I knew until it was time."

"I did everything as if the boarding house was full and functioning normally. The outside light went out automatically at ten-thirty, as did the light across the way at the boys' block. I crept into the bathroom, barefoot, wearing my nightie and knickers, avoiding putting on the light, then climbed onto the toilet, from there onto the windowsill, which was recessed and I could stand on it easily."

"The next bit was tricky as I had to get my left leg over the bottom window while holding the window stay and keep the upper window open while I found the outside ledge with my right leg - difficult because my legs are short and the outside ledge only five inches wide. Then it was a matter of getting my head, right arm and upper body out and then replacing the stay, still in my left hand, to keep the window open. With both legs on the outside window ledge and my fingers grasping the frame of the bottom window I negotiated myself onto the fire escape rail, using the drainpipe between the rail and the window to keep my balance and only letting go when one foot was on the fire escape and both hands could grasp the rail. From there it was an easy matter of creeping down both sets of steps to the ground."

"On a moonlit night it was scary, but with no moonlight to guide me it was terrifying. On that particular night the moon was almost full as I made my way along the wall walking sideways and looking all around me as I went. At the doorway to the boys' block I cut across, crouched down and followed the building wall to Brendon's bathroom window, where I climbed in, trembling with relief. My feet were cold and dirty, and I was about to put them under the bath tap to wash them when the adjoining door opened and there was Brendon, stark naked, his arms out, and moments later I was in his arms, kissing him, trembling with anticipation as he carried me to his bed, not caring about my dirty feet … or anything else."

Chapter 43

"I woke around dawn to find a pair of hazel eyes looking into mine. I was, he said, beautiful when I was asleep, untroubled and peaceful. He also told me that he wanted to always wake up to find me beside him."

"'You must promise you will never leave me, Julie.' he begged, and of course I told him that I never would. 'I don't know how I could live without you.' Then the passion got the better of us and we made love again. I couldn't help but cry out as the climax came, and Brendon whispered that it was just as well nobody could hear me. Much as I wanted to stay, safe and warm with my lover, I had to make tracks back to my bed and did so via the boot room, bolting the door behind me."

"It was safer in daylight to go down to the path which took me past the front of the house, facing the road and under the arch to the boot room. I was far less likely to be seen taking that route. Back in my room, I fell into a deep sleep and was surprised to find that it was mid-morning when I opened my eyes and peered at my clock."

"The other boarders returned during the course of Sunday and I was glad to hear what the girls had all got up to. I am sure they would have been eager to hear how my time had been filled, but obviously this had to remain top secret, although a part of me wanted to take a megaphone out and announce to the world that Brendon and I were lovers."

"We had agreed before I climbed out of his bathroom window that if it was fine, we would meet up on the mound at 5 o clock, and when the time came we met under the apple tree. I leaned against its trunk and said playfully to Brendon that we might pretend we were Adam and Eve, and I reached to pick an apple. I held the apple in front of me and told him what I would do if he managed to get a bite of it. He dropped to his knees opening his mouth and lunging at the apple. As I swung away, teasing him with it just out of reach, I realised that we were not alone. Three of the boys were staring at us, open-mouthed."

"One of them - Adam - said 'Sorry sir, we didn't know you were here.' Brendon assured them that it didn't matter and asked what they were doing, to which Adam replied that they had played tennis earlier and a ball had gone up onto the mound. They were there to look for it. While I stood looking stupid, Brendon said that he had heard them playing, and swearing when the ball went over the top, and thought he would come and look for it himself, with a view to confiscating it as a reprimand. 'Wow, quick thinking!' I thought, and swapped my stupid look for a more relaxed one."

"'I came up to get an apple,' I said, holding up the apple. 'When Mr Ritchie told me he was looking for a tennis ball I said I would help him find it. Shall we get on with it and whoever finds the ball can have the apple?' They were not bothered about the fruit, being boys, and the ball was never found, but they seemed to accept the account of why we were both there on the mound. Phew - that was a close one. It made us realise that we really did have to have a Plan B. And we had to cool things down."

"The last few weeks of term were incredibly frustrating, for me at least. I had been selected for three events in the school's sports day, when all four houses competed for the sports cup. Glossop House must have been desperate because I was not much use (having short legs) for high jump, long jump or the relay race, but my protests fell on deaf ears and I had to just get on with it."

"I had been selected to enter the spoken English competition, too, my reward for coming top of the class in the English exams, so although I dreaded having to stand on stage in front of the whole school in the assembly hall and sound like a poet, again I couldn't pass on that one either.

Then, last and worst, the exams that I was constantly being reminded were to govern my future were looming towards me at great speed."

"I tried to concentrate, tried to revise, tried to care about the impact on my future, but in my mind my future was mapped out. Love, engagement, marriage. Children? Not sure, time would tell."

"My Gran had written to tell me that she had opened the letter from Boots as per my instructions and that they were pleased to confirm that I had secured a position in the pricing department. It stated my start date as Monday August 1st, if that was convenient."

"'So I have to say, Matthew, I really didn't care about school. All I wanted was to leave. Leave school, leave Castle Hill, leave Bakewell, leave my past life and be me, the me I had become and was beginning to like."

"The exams were no worse than I expected. I knew I had done well in the subjects I liked and poorly in the subjects that relied on learning facts that didn't interest me."

"Sports day was embarrassing. Glossop House came third out of the four and I didn't add anything to the scores – eighth in high jump, sixth in long jump and seventh in relay out of a possible eight."

"The spoken English competition was

mortifying. I sat shaking like a leaf till my form teacher asked if I was okay, then they called out my name and up I went shaking even more. I turned to face the audience and opened my mouth. Nothing would come out. The adjudicator tried to calm me saying I should take a deep breath and start again, while smiling at me as if I were a wounded deer. I tried again. Nothing."

"In the end they told me to go back to my seat, where I felt so ashamed that I hid my face in my hands and pretended not to hear the silly comments and noises of my classmates, who found it all so amusing. I can't even remember what poem it was, as I eradicated it from my memory along with the other unpleasant events in my life."

"One thing that *was* enjoyable was getting a prize for being second in my class for the year's exam results. I had to wait for the GCE results, but as I went up on stage again, this time to collect 'The White Peacock' by D H Lawrence which I had chosen for my prize, I saw a look of pride on Brendon's face and a look of absolute shock on the face of the Headmaster. '*Ha!*' I said to myself. '*No sixth form for me, even if you get on your hands and knees and beg!*'

"The last day of term began with assembly, one we had been looking forward to. The whole team of staff members with the exception of the Head and two assistant heads (who probably felt it was inappropriate to give us, the students something to laugh at) entertained us with an array of stand-up comedy, humorous poetry, singing and dancing. Brendon had told me that he was taking part but wouldn't reveal what he was doing, in spite of my constant nagging, pleading, and threats."

"He appeared from the wings wearing a gymslip, bobby socks and oversized replicas of our girls' indoor shoes made from plastic-covered papier maché - a hilarious sight - and when he and two of the female teachers began to sing 'Three Little Maids from School Are We' from Gilbert and Sullivan's Mikado, we could hardly stand up for laughing. With a falsetto which, thankfully, I never heard again, he was the star of the show, and I realised that life with him would be full of fun and laughter."

"So it was goodbye old life and let my new life begin. When the letter arrived asking me what I would like to study for A-levels based on my five passes at O-level, I had great enjoyment writing GET STUFFED on the form and returning it to the Headmaster. Naturally, I didn't tell my Gran what I had done."

Chapter 44

"I collected the addresses of all those I wanted to stay in touch with both at school and at Castle Hill, telephone numbers of those who were lucky enough to have telephones, said my goodbyes, packed my trunk and prepared myself for moving on. The boarders who were flying out to join their families abroad had first call on packing trunks, boarders like myself who weren't travelling far were last to pack. There was a lot more to take back than I had brought with me almost three years ago. I was excited and at the same time a little unsure about the coming change, the rite of passage."

"My trunk was dispatched by train to Beeston where Gramps would collect it from the station, and I caught the bus from Bakewell to Matlock, then Matlock to Derby to Beeston, and made my way to Gran's. I hadn't been able to see or speak to Brendon on the last day, but he had sent me a letter telling me he loved me and couldn't wait to see me. I had given him an envelope with my Gran's writing on it and he copied it expertly to disguise that it was another hand that wrote the letter. It was still posted in Bakewell though, so wouldn't have fooled anyone who suspected a subterfuge."

"In it, he wished me luck with my job and

said he would be in touch very soon. He was staying on at Castle Hill for a few days to tie up some loose ends and was going to look for another teaching post and a flat as Castle Hill was, he said, going to be unbearable without me."

"I had lots to think about, and was glad that I had a couple of weeks to get used to a new way of life. My sixteenth birthday had passed unceremoniously, with a cake and candles, admittedly, and a few cards, one from Harriet with her address and phone number, which of course I knew by heart. A card from Granny to say she was proud of me and my achievements, a big card signed by everyone present in Castle Hill, and a card from Dad, saying he hoped I would come and see him before I started my job and when was he going to meet my boyfriend?"

"Nothing from *her.*"

"Being sixteen didn't seem like a milestone to me anyway, more of an end to having to pretend I was a child. Not any more! I could leave home, even get married. More importantly, I could have *sex* - without fear of discovery, without putting Brendon on the spot."

"Granny greeted me with a big smile, telling me that I was all grown up now and joining the workforce, earning a wage and ready to take whatever life presented me with. We did something that we had never done before or since, except on day trips to the seaside or the countryside, and went out to eat in a restaurant. It was a place in Toton called Grange Farm, where the Council held their banquets and official dinners. I wished that Brendon could have been there with us, but still felt special and enjoyed the meal. It was a treat."

"With all my belongings and a large trunk in the front room of the bungalow, which had been my bedroom any time I wasn't at Castle Hill, there was, as Granny said, no room to swing a cat. A corner cupboard was emptied of glasses and bottles of spirits, unused china and knicknacks, which were consigned to the glory hole that used to be Dad's bedroom instead. Gramps turned the cupboard into a wardrobe with shelves for my record player, records and all the paraphernalia that teenagers accrue. The trunk lived up in the loft, with school stuff in it that I would not revisit for many years."

"I set to making work clothes, aware that wearing the same clothes all week every week was no longer an option, and it gave me a lot of pleasure choosing patterns and fabrics and producing some pretty good outfits with lots of help and advice from Granny. I could knit well and spent the evenings knitting jumpers and cardigans with the telly and stories of Granny's childhood for company when the telly programme was not to our liking."

"I learned a great deal about life in a large family and how much responsibility Granny had been burdened with in looking after seven younger siblings. Her one older sister and brother weren't considered up to the job, and Granny also milked a local farmer's cows on the way to and from school, for a pittance which boosted the family income. She also carded hairnets for a relative with a haberdashery shop and stitched buttons in sets on card for the same relative who also owned a button factory. Her father was a farm labourer, with work seasonal and his income variable, augmented by doing rounds of the local pubs playing his harmonica, telling jokes and singing. Life was busy for the females and the males got off quite lightly, or so it seemed to me."

"The two weeks passed quickly. I did go to see Dad and he gave me ten pounds for my birthday, which I gave to Granny to pay back the loan for dress materials and patterns, cotton, zips and other bits and bobs."

"She and I discussed me looking for a flat or bedsitter locally. I would have to work for a couple of months to save a deposit and Granny said she would take five pounds every week for my bed and board, but she would keep it safe and give it back to me when I had enough for the rent and deposit for a flat. I was looking at about three months before I would be going anywhere. That proved a godsend while I got used to my new routine and I was grateful for the time we spent together."

"Brendon phoned every three or four days and I kept him up to date with all that was happening. His news was a bit of a bombshell, but I realised much later that it was the best option. He had given notice to Lady Manners school and would leave at Christmas."

"He was surprised, he told me, of the reaction to his resignation. Most of his colleagues had said they would be sorry to see him go and the Headmaster had given him a reference which was nothing short of glowing, outlining his excellence as a maths teacher. He would be difficult to replace. He certainly was a good teacher, and well thought of by teachers and pupils alike. He told them that he had been shortlisted for a position with a teacher training college between Bakewell and Sheffield and told me that he was looking into getting a flat in Woodseats in the north of Sheffield."

"Wow! Big changes were on the way."

Chapter 45

"August 1st 1966. My first day as a worker. Dressed in my new skirt and blouse - no cardigan as it was very warm - I drank my tea, ate my Weetabix with jam (not milk), took my potted beef sandwiches, an apple and my favourite chocolate orange Jacob's Club biscuit from Granny (all wrapped in greaseproof paper), put them in my bucket bag and set off - intentionally early as I was unsure of the factory site layout. I had walked the route twice during my two weeks of leisure. Left from Trent Vale Road onto Trent Road, right onto Trafalgar Road, left onto Station Road, right onto Lilac Grove, up to the traffic island and over to the next traffic island, right onto Thane Road and left into the Factory site. I showed my appointment letter to the man on the gate and he opened it and told me to take the next left and go to the end to building D31, which I did with increasing trepidation."

"I reported to the Office Manager. He welcomed me to Boots, told me a brief history of how the company was formed by Jesse Boot, explained what was produced and where, giving me a map of the site and showing me on the map where my office was, the toilets and the canteen. I would be expected to eat there each day, either whatever I had brought with me from home or a meal cooked and bought from the company's kitchen. Then he accompanied me to the office where I would be working."

"It seemed huge, to me. There were rows of desks, rows of comptometers (the early version of a calculator, which printed out your sums on a paper roll), with special chairs, rows of chattering accounting machines and lots of people. I had naively imagined I would be working in a small office with one or two others who would be senior to me. The section I was to work in was, thankfully, on the back wall, and there were just three of us in the pricing section, including myself."

"Ruth was in charge, and I was relieved to find that she looked just like Harriet's mum, bosomy and homely, with a smile that involved her whole face. I knew she would look out for me and not get cross when I made mistakes or didn't know what I was doing. Alice was younger, a Geordie with a wicked sense of humour and a fascinating accent, and you couldn't not like her. So I was lucky."

"Ruth showed me where everything was that I would need. Dockets came to the department and we would find the prices of everything on them from index card files, under different headings. She had prepared a list for me of which heading different items were filed under. Once I had got used to finding them, it would, she said, be a doddle, and in time I would memorise the prices of the most often-used things and be able to recite them in my sleep. Alice told us a funny story about being shaken awake in the night by her husband as she'd been arguing in her sleep about the price of nails, which had gone up that day and which she needed to remember."

"The first day went quickly, with lots to know. Mid-morning a lady came round with a trolley loaded with tea and coffee, and very welcome it was too. At lunchtime we all filed out of the office down to the canteen, which was enormous and smelled lovely. Shepherd's pie, roast meat and vegetables, lovely puddings all carried past me to be eaten hurriedly by the factory workers (and some office staff), who wanted to get outside and smoke a cigarette before returning to the noisy machines that spewed out pills, toothpaste, soap and numerous other products to be shipped to Boots stores."

"I was yawning by 4 o'clock and Alice joked that if I needed a kip, I could curl up in the stationery cupboard, which made me laugh and the moment passed. I was really tired when I walked home and Granny said I looked whacked. It was a lot to take on, she said, but it would get easier, which is just what Brendon said when he phoned to see how my first day had gone. He said we should meet up in Derby on the Saturday and have a day out to celebrate my exam results, my birthday and my new job. Yes, I would really like that, I told him, and asked what he had in mind. He chuckled and said that was for him to know and me to wonder about. I slept like a log."

Chapter 46

"I repeated the same walk every day, thinking I would get Gramps to overhaul my bicycle and get it running now I had located the cycle rack at work. Friday was my day-release at Boots College - in the canteen building, on the same site and virtually next door to my office building. It was one of the few businesses that took an interest in educating teenaged staff."

"The college had been founded by Jesse Boot himself. He was a Nottingham man, born in 1850, and his father had been an agricultural worker but moved to Nottingham and opened a shop there selling herbal remedies. John Boot died when Jesse was only ten, but three years later Jesse began working with his mother, collecting the herbs they needed and running the shop."

"Jesse expanded the business, first by buying medicines at wholesale prices and selling them at a cheaper price than anyone else, and later by dispensing prescription medicine. The business did so well that Jesse began making medicines himself behind the shop."

"In 1885 Jesse was unwell and went to Jersey to recuperate, where he met Florence Rowe – his future wife - at the Wesleyan chapel there. Florence's father was a bookseller and she'd often helped him out in the shop - excellent training for the future Mrs Boot."

"The pair married in August 1886. Jesse's business was already doing very well by then, with several new shops opened outside of Nottingham. But Florence helped it grow even bigger, introducing lending libraries into their shops – right at the back so people had to walk past all the goods on sale - where people could borrow a book for tuppence."

"Florence also helped bring in things like picture framing and the sale of silverware, and by 1914, the Boots empire had grown from ten stores in the East Midlands to over 500 stores across Britain."

"And they were good people, too, Matthew. Jesse Boot is said to have donated more than two million pounds over his lifetime, to charities in Nottingham and Jersey, where Florence was from. And Florence was very committed to the welfare of the workforce at Boot's, especially the women. She set on welfare officers to look after them and made sure they were fed, with breakfasts available for those who wanted them."

"Jesse Boot was knighted for his charity work in 1909 and created Baron Trent in 1917. He was crippled by arthritis, though, so he sold the company in 1920, retiring to Jersey with Florence in 1928, where he died in 1931."

"You sound very interested in these facts, Julie. Why?"

"Well, I benefited from them, Matthew. The company still operated the same principles of developing and caring for its workers that Florence and Jesse had set up. It was largely why Gran thought I should go there."

"The college building was built in the 1930s, just as the war was about to kick off, and designed to be turned into a military hospital if it should suddenly become needed. So it was huge, and the canteen took up most of the ground floor, though by the time I got there some of it had been walled off for a data processing centre - D31. This is where my office was – the Cost Department – and also the General Services Department and Boots College.

"Interesting, Julie, and to think I've never heard of it! Is it still there?"

"No, I think they closed the college in about 1969. D31 building was closed in 2006. They opened a Boots museum, though, on the mezzanine floor at the end of the building. That was in the 1990s, I think."

"But the college was flourishing when I was there in 1966 and it did a lot to make me the person I am today."

"How, Julie?"

"By teaching me skills I'd need in everyday

life, not just the workplace. The idea was the college would ease the step for their young people from school to work, focus them on their skills and ambitions, help them into an adult world where their learning wasn't monitored and where exercise was fun and not competitive. The syllabus was both unusual and innovative, with classes of between 10 to 14 pupils. I was used to being in a class of 30 or more. The company had taken on many of the immigrant population, and the basic English classes the college ran were popular and useful to them. As for me, I was able to hone up my maths and learn about managing money, banking and the aspects of mathematics that are useful in day-to-day living."

"I learned to cook there, too - after a shaky start, but more about that later! Having left a school where I'd learned a lot about sewing and nothing about cooking, I'd now had the misfortune of starting at a new school where cookery was the focus and needlework would take over next term. I had done some cookery with Granny, but on reflection it was the frills and fancy work I did while she did most of the preparation."

"I enjoyed archery at the Boots College, even won the Robin Hood prize at the end of term. Trampolining had been a luxury at Lady Manners, only available when supervisors could

242

be found, which wasn't often. At Boots College I gained two certificates in 'rebound tumbling' as it was known then, and I enjoyed it immensely. The College wasn't an educational institution per se, but definitely a bonus to all young people who wanted to apply to Boots for a job."

"Now I will tell you about my experience of cookery, Matthew. We - a class of about 10 girls - were told each week which ingredients to bring the following week. There was a recipe in each place setting and a list of the equipment that we would need and which we took out of the store cupboard. This particular day the dish was to be apple pie. I read the instructions: grease a baking tray, cut the butter into small pieces and rub into the flour until the mixture resembles fine breadcrumbs. Okay, done that."

"I was startled by a loud voice in my left ear saying, 'Julie Brady, whatever DO you think you are doing?' Puzzled, I looked at the instructions and pointed to the bit about mixing the butter and flour.

'You do NOT mix the butter and flour on a baking sheet! Silly girl, you use a bowl! Do you know ANYTHING at all about cookery?' the teacher asked, critically.

'Well no, actually, I don't. And it doesn't say on the sheet that that is what you do.' That made the girls laugh!"

"The teacher gaped at me, her mouth opening and shutting but with nothing coming out. Then she shook her head, tutted, and every week after that she came and asked me if I understood the task and what was involved. I should have been mortified, but it soon turned into an act which the whole class joined in with and eventually even the teacher saw the funny side of it. Needless to say, I was very careful to check it out with Granny before setting off on Friday mornings. She and Gramps were pleased with my offerings, too, and it gave Granny a bit of a break from cooking."

Chapter 47

"So, Julie. This was goodbye old life, hello new life?"

"Yes Matthew. This was the new me, an adult, with a job, a boyfriend, everything to look forward to, on the brink of freedom."

"Did it not scare you just a little bit?"

"If I could deal with my scary past, the future had no fears for me. I was in control now and I wasn't going to let anything or anyone take away another thing from me, or harm me in any way."

"Did you truly believe that was possible?"

"Yes, I did. With hindsight I would have advised caution, but that had never been part of my character, and I still wasn't sure whether or not I deserved the bad things that had happened to me. Now that I had someone to love, who loved me back, I didn't need much else."

"Life continued in the same pattern for the next six months. I would catch a train to Sheffield on Saturdays, returning late Saturday night, and Brendon and I would also meet up in Derby on a Tuesday or Wednesday. There was no question of living together 'over the broom', 'in sin' or as a kept woman in those days, but we spent most Saturdays in Brendon's flat in Woodseats, enjoying ourselves in every possible way as lovers do, and we got to know each other's quirks and foibles very well."

"The first time I visited his flat, Brendon and I were on a real high. We couldn't wait to get our clothes off and get into bed. As we were totally unencumbered by fear of discovery, we let the moment take over and were pretty wild with our lovemaking. It was brought to an end by a pain which took my breath away, and when Brendon withdrew, concerned that he may have unintentionally hurt me, there was blood on his sheets. We panicked until the pain went away, but were both worried. I decided to see Dr Frost a.s.a.p. and made an appointment for the following week. He examined me and informed me that I was no longer technically a virgin as my hymen had ruptured. It had been intact on the last examination, in spite of the fact that I had been sexually abused, and had also entered into a sexual relationship recently. He said my hymen must have been made of strong stuff!!"

"I relayed all of this to Brendon from a phone box - it was not something I could do at my Gran's. He was very relieved, and I was pleased that he had been the one to do the deed."

"Brendon had a few faults. He tended towards hypochondria, always fearful that he might be ill, probably because his parents were not in the best of health, but then they were approaching sixty, which was considered old in the 1960s."

"He was a railway fanatic, always interested in memorabilia of the steam era and a collector of loco plates and numbers, British Rail signs, anything that resulted from the 1965 Beeching closure of fifty-five percent of the country's train stations and thirty percent of route miles of railway line. This had been done with a view to increasing efficiency, stemming the large losses being incurred during a period of increasing competition from road transport and reducing the rail subsidies necessary to keep the network running. Protests resulted in the saving of *some* stations and lines, but the majority were closed as planned. A few of these routes have since reopened - some short sections preserved as Heritage railways, while others have been incorporated into the National Cycle Network, such as the Tissington Trail; some have undergone reconstruction, some have reverted to farmland, or remain derelict."

"I believe Bakewell has become part of the Tissington Trail. It's something my boys would enjoy, riding their bikes along an old railway line. Carry on, Julie."

"Brendon took every opportunity to follow the progress of the demolition and we often spent a Saturday visiting newly disenfranchised stations, Brendon recording on camera the sights that were soon to be lost. You may be wondering why I list it as a fault, Matthew. It was really an obsession, and if his nose was in a book or magazine, it was always railway orientated, and there was little of discussion value in it as I knew very little about railway matters. I much preferred to go walking in Derbyshire, which mostly started at Fox House Inn on the Sheffield to Hathersage road - on the map, it is named Houndkirk Road - as most of the walks could begin and end there."

"The Inn had been part of the Longshaw estate since 1773. Apparently, it was first called 'The Traveller's Rest' but then it was renamed after a local landowner called George Fox. Many of our walks from Fox House were to the Burbage Valley, which is a sweeping curved valley in the Dark Peak with a gorgeous brook flowing the length of it. To the south the brook flows through the Padley Gorge - it's beautiful. And then there are crags and woodland which are very pleasant indeed. We tried to do one of the walks there most weekends, usually on a Sunday."

"So did Brendon find a new teaching post?"

"He got the job at the teacher training college, which involved more assessment than teaching children and marking homework. Often by Friday night he was too tired to spend the evening doing written evaluations and advice, so, if he was visiting his parents on Sunday, it meant spending some time without interruption working on these on Saturday. I was fairly good most of the time, knitting, sewing, reading, listening to records or watching television on low volume, but I did resent taking a back seat, and sometimes resorted to some pretty extreme behaviour to get his attention."

"I had a sexy black negligee which I kept at the flat and I would nip out of the lounge, where Brendon was working at the table at the far end by the window, get undressed and creep back to the lounge, switch off the light and wrap myself around him, cover him with kisses and rub his shoulders and neck, to relieve the tension in them. By then I was hard to resist, and you can imagine the rest, Matthew."

"If it didn't work, I was narky and we would part on a bad note. That didn't happen too often though, and if it did, one of us would phone on the next day to apologise."

"Did you have any time with other people, Julie, pursue other interests?"

"I was very much into the pop scene, films and theatre, and often had to go straight from a cinema or the Crucible theatre to the station to get back to Beeston. We both neglected our friends to be together, but all in all we had some really good times and made some beautiful memories."

"Back in Beeston, Granny and I had time to share housework and talk about many things. Dad sometimes came over on a Sunday and kept us informed as to what was happening in his world. My brother Michael was returning home to Canal Street at Christmas and Billy had been taken into care in his first term at school, diagnosed as neglected and unable to integrate socially with other children. Dad's divorce hearing was in October and he got a decree nisi, which would become a decree absolute in 2 years."

"We talked about the breakup of the family and I asked Dad straight out why he had married *her*. It's not as if she'd been pregnant. She had boasted that *he* had been keen on starting 'before the whistle blew', which she had no intention of allowing. I don't think she was interested in sex anyway, Matthew, and I never saw any sign of affection from her to my dad."

"I knew the real answer. He was trying to rescue her. He admitted that he knew there were parts of her personality which rang alarm bells in him, even before they got married, but he genuinely thought that taking her out of a bad situation and loving her would change those elements. We all know that anyone who believes that they can change someone's personality is sadly disillusioned, but that will never stop some of us from trying."

"I asked Dad what he meant by 'change those elements.' When pushed to expand on the bits of her personality that alarmed him, he said that the real *her* had emerged when I was around six months old and wouldn't sleep for more than half an hour during the daytime. She resented this, and the fact that I was getting mobile, needing attention, solid food, and things to play with. He said that was when it all went pear-shaped. She was, *she* said, more at home in an office."

"Granny said she had told Dad that *she* wouldn't make a good wife and mother and that he would be better off with Enid, and of course, Granny was proved right. Dad added that when his mum's offers of help came, *she* was furious, and took it out on him and on me, and without Granny's intervention in notifying the Authorities who had put me in care, he didn't think I would've been alive today."

Chapter 48

"That last revelation of yours was a bit drastic, Julie. Did your dad think she might have actually killed you?"

"Possibly. She did some awful things to him, Matthew, including getting my brother to shoot the end of Dad's finger off with an air rifle. Yes, I think it's possible. I ended up in hospital on several occasions after she'd given me a beating. But there was no Child Protection Agency in the 1950's."

"It's no wonder you wanted nothing to do with her with the way she treated you. That would have psychological effects on your mental health, too."

"Yes, it did. I didn't want children of my own in case I had the gene that would make me behave like *her*."

"Understandable. But you have two children, don't you?"

"Yes, Matthew, I do. I was almost 32 when I had my first and 34 when I had the second, and I knew as soon as I held them both that I would go to the ends of the earth for them, even die for them, and I would always protect them. I never let them out of my sight until they were old enough to have earned some freedom. I loved them with every bit of me, and thoroughly enjoyed being with them. I was fortunate enough to be a stay-at-home Mum, and I relived my own childhood by being part of theirs."

"I honestly don't know how *she* could shove me out the door and not care where I went, who I was with, and what might happen to me."

"It's pretty rare to find that level of neglect. Did your father know what was going on?"

"My grandma did, and she told him about it, but Dad wasn't prepared to take action, and that's why she stepped in. Granny had begged to have me live with her and grandpa, but to no avail. Dad's inaction has coloured my opinion of men throughout my life and I have had great difficulty trusting men to do the right thing for most of my life."

"Hardly surprising, I would say! You believed in Brendon, though?"

"Oh yes. He was different. Well, I believed he was different."

"So tell me what happened next."

"Although I had planned to get a flat or bedsitter, I ended up staying at Granny's for a year and a few months, seeing Brendon mid-week and Saturdays, and occasionally Sundays. I had to lie to do this, by telling Granny that Brendon and I were staying with his parents on a Saturday night."

"We did that sometimes, but it was so

marvellous being able to spend a whole night together in his flat and go for long walks on Sunday. My job was proving easier, so life was getting so much better."

"We decided that we would get engaged and Brendon went to Fattorini's in Sheffield to choose a ring, which he presented to me on my 17th birthday. He asked me to marry him and of course, I said yes!"

"At the beginning of autumn there was an epidemic of flu which hit the Boots' Pricing Department and most of the Accounts machine operators were laid up at home. The office manager took a number of us from our usual posts and trained us on the accounts machines. I was chosen as I was the junior in my section. I liked the change."

After a week of working in Accounts I was called into the Manager's office. I took a deep breath and knocked on his door in trepidation, expecting to be criticised for poor work. I was amazed, then, when he smiled at me and said that not only was my work accurate, but I had the best accuracy record they had ever seen, even among the regular staff, with a 98% success rate on balancing the books. I knew that I could transcribe numbers well, but that was music to my ears. He said that if I was willing, I could remain in Accounts and would qualify for a pay rise."

"Of course I was willing, and I spent the day on cloud nine. I was able to see Maxine, Ruth and Alice from Pricing on tea breaks and lunchtimes, and they were happy for me. They'd been told that I would be replaced with another school leaver, but it didn't happen for the remainder of my time at Boots."

"I had been working for Boots for a year and was beginning to want to settle down. Beeston wasn't where I wanted to be - Sheffield was."

"Granny and I talked about it. She said that she thought Brendon and I would make a good marriage, and she could understand me wanting to spend more time with him. It was, she said, important to know as much as possible about the man you're going to marry before the event. But she said we mustn't live together as man and wife until we *were* man and wife."

"It seems so very old fashioned nowadays, when young couples move in together after a few weeks of dating, but she *was* old fashioned. She'd made a good job of being married to the same man for almost fifty years, not because everything was perfect between them, but because they talked about decisions to be made, and when there was disagreement, they reached a compromise. Where there was no choice - for instance, when they couldn't have more children after my dad's birth - they accepted it and didn't put the blame on each other, but filled their lives doing much to help less fortunate folk and improving their community."

"Granny said that she hoped that I, her granddaughter, would prove better than my parents at holding things together, in spite of having no good role models, only bad experiences of how not to treat family. I assured her that she was the best role model and the best grandmother a girl could wish for. We had a little cry and a hug, and promised each other that we would always care and be there for each other, no matter what turned up."

"Granny had saved almost £300 in 'board money' and she said I could take it to set me up in Sheffield. I insisted that she keep half of it, and she said it would be banked in a T.S.B savings account in my name in case I ever needed it. She was so wise, Matthew, it's almost as if she had a sixth sense and could see what was coming."

"Although your parents let you down, Julie, you were fortunate to have the grandparents that you had. Not everybody is as fortunate."

"I know, Matthew, and I thank God for them."

"Brendon was really pleased when I told him that I would be joining him in Sheffield. He said he would find me lodgings, look at jobs being advertised in the local paper and phone me as soon as he had found one or both. True to his word, he phoned a couple of days later to say he'd found an elderly lady with a room to let in Woodseats and he had details of three possible jobs. I discounted two of them as I thought they were looking for someone more experienced. I wrote to the third, a firm running a rental business in Walkley, saying I was interested in being part of the team of accounts machinists. I received a reply offering me an interview and arranged to take a day off work to go to Sheffield, where I would meet my landlady, too. It was exciting, and also a little scary, but for Brendon and I to be together it was going to be worth the upheaval."

"The day came and I caught an early train to Sheffield, got a bus to Walkley and headed for Whitehouse Road. The bus driver gave me directions and I found it easily. I was shocked to find that the building was - or had been - a Methodist Chapel, and later discovered it was called St Saviours. It was in fairly bad condition and was cold and gloomy. Nonetheless, I had my interview with a rather elderly office manager, who told me what was entailed, should I choose to accept the job."

"I wasn't over impressed with the setup, but

the wage was good - less than I would be earning in Beeston, but the cost of living was considerably less in Sheffield. So I said yes, I would accept the job, and would give the required two weeks' notice to Boots."

"I had to hang around to see Daisy about the room in Woodseats, so I familiarised myself with the city centre, had lunch in the British Home Stores restaurant, and caught the bus to Woodseats, then headed for Brendon's flat where he would meet me at 5:30. We went together to Daisy's house on Tyzack Road, only five minutes' walk away. It turned out that Daisy wasn't her given name, which was Iris, but everybody called her Daisy. She said I would be welcome to the room she had vacant and would charge me three pounds ten shillings a week, to include breakfast and a packed sandwich lunch. I would eat my evening meal with Brendon. So it was all sorted - in just over two weeks my new life would begin."

"We went to the local pub to celebrate and had fish and chips on the way back to Brendon's flat, after which we celebrated with what would soon become a regular form of exercise, before we headed for the station."

Chapter 49

"Good morning Julie. How did the move to Sheffield go?"

"Gramps got down my trunk from the attic and I set to, wiping off a year's dust, then filling it with my accumulated clothes, vinyl records - mostly LP's - my radio, record player, books and personal effects, all the time thinking that in a few days I would have everything I ever wanted, someone to love and to be loved by, my own Brendon. It was overwhelming and I actually found tears coming, to my surprise, but tears of happiness."

"Thinking about all the things we could do together made my heart sing and filled the days till my notice was worked. I had decided to go up to Sheffield on the train, straight from work on Friday, to give me the weekend to get straight."

"Saying goodbye to Granny was hard. We had grown to love each other deeply, and we genuinely enjoyed being together, always having lots to talk about, and for me, that time we had was my growing up time. But it was time to grow up elsewhere and she understood that this was a crossroads in my life where I chose the road to take and had to live with that choice."

"Brendon would meet me and my trunk at Sheffield station and we would get a taxi from the station to his flat. I was going to leave my trunk in his spare room alongside his railway memorabilia, and take what I needed to Tyzack Road in several trips. My plan was to go straight to the flat each day from work and stay till around 10 pm when Brendon would walk me 'home'. I had told Daisy that I would be going home to my Gran's regularly and that was the intention. When it offered a chance to stay overnight at the flat, we had to hope that we would not be spotted in Woodseats when I was supposed to be in Beeston."

"So you lied to Daisy, then?"

"Not intentionally, but it was too tempting to stay with Brendon. And I did go back to Beeston a few times."

"I started work on the Monday, having spent the weekend making space in the flat for things like my books and records and record player, shopping for food and trying to impress Brendon with my newly acquired cookery skills. We looked at the programmes for the Crucible Theatre and the local cinemas and decided what we would like to see. Brendon decided to take driving lessons with a view to getting a car. Life was exciting."

"I joined the library at the bottom of Bromwich Road turning left onto Chesterfield Road. It was at this time that the Liverpool Scene was turning out groups like The Scaffold of Lily the Pink fame. The Scaffold were a comedy, poetry and music trio from Liverpool, consisting of musical performer Mike McGear - whose real name was Peter Michael McCartney and was the brother of Paul McCartney, the poet Roger McGough and comic entertainer John Gorman. I immersed myself in the Liverpool culture where I found the poet Adrian Henri, who was completely nuts. I also started reading Roger McGough."

"My favourite poem of Roger's was 'Let Me Die a Youngman's Death.' My favourite verse was,

> *Let me die a youngman's death*
> *not a free from sin tiptoe in*
> *candle wax and waning death*
> *not a curtains drawn by angels borne*
> *'what a nice way to go' death.'*[1]

"Adrian Henri performed live with his group 'The Liverpool Scene.' My favourite poem of his is called 'Love Is,' and my favourite two verses go -

---

[1] McGough, Roger – in the public realm on https://www.poetry.com/poem/53911/let-me-die-a-youngman's-death

'Love is fish and chips on winter nights
Love is blankets full of strange delights
Love is when you don't put out the light
Love is

Love is you and love is me
Love is a prison and love is free
Love's what's there when you're away from me
Love is…"[2]

"I used to go to the library and read all these whilst I was waiting for Brendon to come home - from the Library I would see the light come on in his flat. For me they embodied the sixties and I felt I had so much to be grateful for, living in these times."

"Brendon was sold on the Dave Brubeck Quartet, a jazz band whose 'muzac' made me want to bang my head against the wall till it hurt more than listening to jazz did."

"We differed largely on music tastes. I loved the happy vibe of the Beach Boys and the Byrds, most pop music and daft stuff like The Scaffold. I loved to dance, adored dancing to Reggae – Bob Marley especially, felt very much at home with Tamla Motown and even liked Folk Music, Steeleye Span, Fairport Convention, Bob Dylan,

[2] Henri, Adrian, in the public realm on
https://www.adrianhenri.com/poem-love-is

Joni Mitchell and Joan Baez to name but a few. I went out with the girls at work sometimes and we often ended up in the nightclubs, dancing till dawn, and on these occasions I told Brendon he didn't need to cook for me and I crept into number 19 Tyzack Road using my key, trying to avoid tripping over Daisy's smelly cat, which had an uncanny way of knowing I was coming home late."

"Work was bearable, but everything about it was shabby. The owners - two brothers - were mean with every possible commodity; we girls felt better after writing some awful poems about their stinginess and passing them round the staff, it was the only thing we had to smile about. One day my engagement ring slipped off my finger and fell down a gap in the floorboards, causing me much distress and only the ingenuity of one of the reps along with a wire coat hanger and a whole afternoon of 'fishing' - with guards posted at the door in case the bosses were heading our way - managed to restore the ring to my finger. That was the day I decided I needed a better job."

"Also, it involved catching two buses each way and a lot of standing at bus stops. I wanted to work in the city."

"Speaking of buses, my periods had started to become painful again. The pills had stopped being effective pain relief and I was having heavy loss and pain which caused me to pass out again. On several occasions I was carried off the bus and ambulanced to Sheffield Royal Infirmary, where I had to wait for Brendon to take me home."

"Brendon was very good at looking after me, and was concerned about my health, but I believe that a lot of the problem was from not drinking enough. The toilets at work were abominable and though tea breaks were twice a day, we made our own drinks and washed up afterwards that took most of the 10 minutes allowed. So I didn't drink unless I really needed to. I did discover the benefits of Indian Brandy though."

"Did you not go to see a doctor, Julie?"

"No Matthew, I relied on Brendon for pretty much everything. I had a problem with my wisdom teeth, they were growing outwards instead of upwards and downwards, making my cheeks and gums sore and ulcerated and I had to find a dentist quickly. When I went to have the teeth taken out, they did it with nitrous oxide as pain relief, otherwise known as laughing gas. I was sedated, but came round halfway through the procedure, causing panic and mayhem when I saw the bloodbath, and tried to escape the building while laughing hysterically and having to be restrained before being given a second dose of the anaesthetic. They had to ring Brendon at work and get him to fetch me as I had nobody else I could ask to escort me home. What a pain I was!"

"Who said you were a pain?"

"Me!"

That made Matthew smile. "No comment."

Chapter 50

"I started to look in the Sheffield Star for a better job and within a couple of weeks I found one. There was a wholesale grocers on Shalesmoor who wanted an accounts clerk to 'look after' the Mace grocers in the area. I applied and was given an interview date. I took an afternoon as annual leave and found out the bus times from Woodseats and from Walkley and turned up on the day, to be amazed at the size and grandeur of the building, both inside and out."

"The receptionist rang the office manager who came down, shook my hand and took me back up the stairs to his office. He was pleasant – both to look at and in his manners - and spent an hour and a half asking me about me, where I lived, my work experience, what I enjoyed doing in my spare time. Then he explained what was involved in the clerk's job, and at the end of the interview said he would let me know if I had been successful as he had some more applicants to see."

"As he said this he winked at me, which I found disconcerting. He showed me the office where I would be working and introduced me to Margaret, a mature lady with a daughter a little younger than myself, and Sandra, a fairly quiet and shy girl a little older than me who operated an accounting machine identical to the one at what might become my desk. He started a conversation with Margaret, which I wasn't listening to, until Sutton-in-Ashfield was mentioned and I realised that that was where he lived. Only of interest because that was where Brendon's parents lived, too."

"Going straight back to the flat, I was surprised to find Brendon at home, due, he explained, to fire training for his students which freed him of his afternoon lectures. We had a cup of tea and he asked how the interview had gone. I told him that I thought the job was in the bag and that the office manager lived in Sutton-in-Ashfield."

"'I doubt if I'd know him but what's his name?' asked Brendon.

'Daniel Bailey,' I replied. Brendon's face changed just a shade with a hint of a frown.

'What does he look like?"

'Tallish, blonde curly hair, square jaw, well built ...'

'Like a rugby player?'

'Yes, now you mention it. Do you know him?'

'Hah, do I know him? He was the bane of my life at school. I wasn't sporty at all, unlike Dan and his mates. He was Dan the Man and I was Brenda Boffin.'"

"I exploded with laughter. 'He called you Brenda Boffin? Honestly?'

'I'm glad you find it amusing!' Brendon said and stomped off to the kitchen, taking the teacups."

"I left it a couple of minutes while I straightened my face then went after him. He was standing with his back to me looking out of the kitchen window, arms folded, shoulders slumped forward and he wasn't a happy bunny. I said I was sorry for laughing, put my arms round him and did my best to cheer him up. I said I would treat him to steak and chips and a bottle of wine later in the evening, and by then he was more amenable. We agreed that we wouldn't discuss Dan the Man again, and I said I probably wouldn't get the job anyway."

"I was wrong. I did get the job and I accepted it. I figured that fifteen years had gone by since Brendon had been teased by Daniel and it should be assigned to the past, where it belonged."

"Time went by. Brendon took his driving test and passed, then bought a green Morris Minor which made it possible to walk where we chose to walk, no longer restricted to bus routes and timetables. We often went back to the hills and dales of Derbyshire, but managed to steer clear of Bakewell."

"My 18th birthday was approaching and Brendon had plans for celebrating it. I nipped into the city at lunchtime - a 5 minute walk - and bought a lovely dress from Wallis's. I changed into it just before 5 pm and Brendon picked me up from work soon after that. We drove out onto the moors and ate venison in a cosy restaurant with a bottle of red wine and Black Forest gateau for dessert. Then we drove to a pub that Brendon knew and met up with some friends of his and we celebrated the fact that I could now legally drink alcohol in a pub."

"I had been drinking in pubs and restaurants since I was 15 and nobody had ever challenged me about my age as I looked considerably older. Fortunately, I didn't look more than 18 till I was 35."

"I got a bit silly and asked for a whisky chaser. I had heard about it on the telly or on a bus and thought it sounded very swish. Brendon raised his eyebrows when I asked for a third whisky chaser, but I assured him that I was fine. After the fourth one, the bell on the bar called time and we headed for home. I walked to the car, noting how mild the weather was, but that wasn't surprising as it was mid–July. Daisy thought I had gone home for my birthday and the weekend, so it was going to be a night of passion at the flat."

"When we arrived at the flat I climbed the 21 steps to the front door, and then halfway up the stairs from the door to the first floor I started to take off my clothes. I was down to my underwear when Brendon scooped me up and carried me to the bedroom. As he laid me on the bed the room began to swim. I muttered 'I love you,' and remember nothing until I woke with a raging thirst at around five the next morning. I staggered to the kitchen, rinsed out a milk bottle, filled it with cold water and swigged the whole pint down, then went back to bed, feeling distinctly weird."

"Brendon woke me up at 7:30 with a cup of tea and the question - was I feeling okay and what would I like for breakfast? My stomach did a somersault and I felt the blood drain from my head. I said I was okay but didn't want any breakfast, I would grab something in the canteen at coffee break. Almost retching, I cleaned my teeth, put on yesterday's work clothes and headed for the bus stop."

"By the time I arrived at work my head was spinning, the office seemed to be spinning in the opposite direction and I was staggering alarmingly. Margaret and Sandra made some black coffee and did their best to keep 'visitors' at bay, but the word had got around that Julie from accounts was drunk as a skunk and eventually it filtered through to Daniel Bailey, who came to see for himself and proceeded to admonish me for the state I was in. When he couldn't keep it up any longer, he burst out laughing and asked if I had looked in the mirror. I could see the funny side when I did, but I was by now feeling really ill."

"Daniel got one of the delivery men to take me home to the flat and said I was not to come back to work until I was in a fit state. I went back to bed with a glass of water and some Phensic pills and slept till mid-afternoon, when I got up and made a marmalade sandwich. I ate the sandwich very slowly and was still eating it, watching the television, when Brendon came home."

"He wasn't surprised to see me and said that he didn't know how I had managed to get to work. He also said that it was not a pretty sight, and he hoped I would not be making a habit of getting drunk. If I had felt better I would have given him a hard time, but I kept quiet and went to work the following morning."

Chapter 51

"A few weeks later all was forgiven and we went to the cinema in Heeley – I can't remember what we went to see, but it was a good film. As we were leaving, a voice behind said 'hello, Brendon!' and I was mortified to see my form master from Lady Manners School with his wife. He said 'hello, Julie' and didn't seem at all surprised to see me with Brendon. I didn't know where to look, what to say, and just wanted the floor to open up and swallow me whole."

"He looked at us both and even Brendon looked a bit sheepish, then he laughed and said he wasn't surprised that we were together. He was a keen stargazer and while training his telescope on the sky above Castle Hill, had seen what appeared to be a ghost on the fire escape on several occasions. His house was off the Monyash Road, one of the highest points in Bakewell. He'd never told anyone of his sightings, but had suspected that something extra curricular might be going on. We all laughed about it and said we must meet up sometime. No way ever in my life would that happen, I thought to myself, and we slunk away home grateful for his silence."

"Did you make many friends in Sheffield, Julie?"

"Not really, Matthew, just the people I worked with. I kept in touch with Harriet and went to Grindleford a couple of times when Brendon was off somewhere for the weekend and Granny and Gramps were away or busy, but I never felt the need for friends. Also, I have to say that I was not good at forming friendships, as it seemed that every child that I made friends with disappeared out of my life for one reason or another, mainly because of the transitional nature of my childhood. I still find myself weighing up whether to get involved with people, generally finding that the fear of failing people and the pain of separation add up to too big a price to pay."

"Yes, it's a form of anxiety which results from fear of abandonment, and it's common in children who were neglected or haven't formed a bond with the important people in their lives, like mothers and fathers. We can talk about this later."

"Brendon did keep in touch with the older boys from Castle Hill and we were surprised when one of them, Adrian, got in touch with him regarding a reference for a job he had applied for. I was even more surprised to hear that he and Lisa (who'd shared my dormitory at Castle Hill), were an item. It turned out that they too had begun a relationship in their last weeks at school and were now virtually engaged."

"We invited them for dinner on the next Saturday evening, and I was looking forward to seeing them and catching up. I decided to cook the meal, Brendon would sort out drinks. They were coming by train and Brendon would pick them up from the station. I decided to cook a steak pie and serve it with carrots peas and mashed potatoes."

"On the day, I bought the ingredients and laid them out on the small Formica table which served as a worktop and breakfast table. Brendon got out his best cutlery - at least, knives and forks that matched - and uncorked the wine to 'breathe' and set the dining table in the lounge. We'd bought place mats, serviettes and glasses from the second-hand shop – it was before they were renamed charity shops – and I began the cooking."

"Remembering the disaster that was my first attempt at making pastry, I had written down everything I needed to do. Weigh the flour, sieve it, add a pinch of salt. Weigh equal measures of Trex and margarine and rub it into the flour (in a bowl!!!) till the mixture resembles breadcrumbs. Add enough water to make a firm dough and leave it in a cool place to rest. Brendon's flat had no fridge, but the pantry cupboard was on an outside wall and kept food cool and fly-free. Peel the potatoes, scrape the carrots, open a tin of Batchelor's garden peas. Leave the spuds and carrots in cold water till needed."

"After a cup of tea and a nibble of the Twiglets, we started to watch the TV, till I realised that time was marching on and our guests would arrive in less than an hour. I finely chopped an onion to go with the steak, lit the oven, then turned my attention to the pastry. By the time I had rolled it out, cut the base for the pie dish and a smaller circle for the top, with only one or two patches, where it resisted being stretched into the dish, Brendon was ready to go and collect Adrian and Lisa."

"I spooned in the steak and onion and carefully placed the pastry top over the meat, pricking the pastry artistically with a fork. I even managed to use the leftover pastry to cut some leaves as decoration. In the oven it went for 40 minutes, and I started to clear up. Twenty minutes later we were all sat drinking sherry and chatting away."

"Suddenly there was an overpowering smell of burning pastry. I dashed to the kitchen, rescued the pie, put the carrots and potatoes on to boil, scraped as much of the black stuff off the pie as I could without making holes and I served up the worst steak pie in the world with undercooked potatoes and carrots. The peas were forgotten in the panic, and I realised that Brendon didn't have a potato masher - just as well as the potatoes were only half-cooked."

"When we cut into the pie the meat was grey and rubbery, the blood had run into the pastry on the bottom which was soggy, and I had not thought about gravy. We all looked at one another until Brendon said that the pie wasn't edible and he would go and get fish and chips. So we drank the Nuits St George with our fish and chips and laughed about it. I never made another meat pie without cooking the meat first."

Chapter 52

"We decided late in the Summer that we would like to go on holiday together, and we thought the Lake District would be a good choice. I had told Brendon about going on the school trip, and he bought Ordnance Survey maps and traced all the places I had been. He made some phone calls and amazingly, Bassenthwaite Manor - which had been the youth hostel when I was twelve - had been bought privately and turned into a hotel."

"I was excited to see how it looked now, and Brendon was enthusiastic about the walking, spending many hours poring over his maps and library books with suggested walking routes. I bought walking boots, socks, shorts and tee shirts, and counted the days down to our little adventure."

"At last the day came and we loaded up the car with all-weather walking gear and our best clothes for evening wear and set off in Maurice (the green Morris Minor), stopping on the way to eat our packed lunch and buy teas and coffees, use the loo and stretch our legs. We arrived in Bassenthwaite mid-afternoon."

"I won't bore you with the whole itinerary, but the hotel was magnificent, the scruffy areas, made scruffy by years of children in muddy boots had been tidied up and repurposed, but the dining room and the games room were exactly as they had been and I was tickled pink when we were shown to our room and it was the same room with the same view as when I shared it with three girls in my class at school!"

"Brendon and I spent most evenings in the bar, and it seemed to be the place where the gentlemen, mostly middle aged or elderly, congregated to down a pint and smoke a pipe or cigarettes. I found myself quite the centre of attention, and this made Brendon very protective and attentive and he showed me lots of affection. Of course, here he wasn't bogged down with work, marking and assessing and the rest. I lapped it up anyway."

"We visited some places familiar to me, walked all the way round Derwent Water and went out on Windermere in a river cruiser. Brendon found a mountain that not many people know about, called Robinson, and we climbed all the way up and were astonished to find that most of the lakes were visible from this vantage point. It was truly spectacular, and I realised that I was holding my breath in awe and wonder. We sat back to back, holding each other up and soaked up the sun and the ambience."

"We were alone, we didn't see a soul all day. I closed my eyes and found myself floating in the space between sky and mountain and yet I could see my body next to Brendon's on the rocks. I was held in some kind of out of body experience, and a wave of pure joy ran through me like fire in my veins. I didn't want to come back to earth but a voice was in my head, telling me that I was safe and loved and watched over by angels. I shook myself and found Brendon looking at me strangely. I assumed he had said that I was safe, and I said that I was really touched by his words. He said I must have been dreaming as he had said nothing. I told him about the out of body experience and he laughed, saying I was half asleep."

"I began to wonder then about what it meant, but I had no idea that I was indeed safe and loved and watched over by angels. It took 18 years to find this out."

"That sounds amazing, Julie. I can't wait to hear about that."

Chapter 53

"All too soon it was time to go home. We talked about our wedding on the way back from the Lakes and Brendon said he would organise a meeting with the Vicar of the local church. There were many reasons why we chose Sheffield and not Sutton-in-Ashfield or Beeston, and it would be a small affair."

"I had received a letter, redirected from Granny, which was unexpected. It was from Lindsey, a girl I had befriended at Long Eaton Grammar school."

"She had been sent to live with her aunt in Long Eaton, as her mother had had a crisis of mental health. We called it a nervous breakdown in those days, Matthew, which seems to me to be a more accurate description of what has happened, but anyway Lindsey came to the Grammar school and seemed so sad that I just wanted to put a smile on her face. I knew better than to ask her what the problem was, even at 13 years old, and there were quite a few of my age group going through the teenage blues – not children, not adults, but adolescents in a world which didn't cater for mood swings and feelings of rage, despair, fear, inability to slot into any role expected of them. All these feelings were written so clearly on Lindsey's face, and most of her classmates avoided her as they would a plague."

"By degrees and by offering to help her navigate round the school timetable and the building, she let her guard down enough for us to be friends."

"Ellen was prepared to allow her into our twosome and now we were three, although Ellen didn't find her as fascinating as I did. After one term I started to visit her at her aunt's house and we would go for long walks, either along the canal towards Ilkeston or along the River Soar to Trent Lock, where the River Soar meets the River Trent. Her aunt was pleased to have her own children to herself, and gladly made sandwiches for us both."

"I learned that Lindsey was as insecure as I was, which made it so much easier to identify and empathise with her, and she and I swapped tales of neglect and bullying, negative thoughts and self-loathing, all the mental abuse and lack of love that made our self-esteem sink into oblivion. We had a bond. We totally understood each other. We promised to be friends forever, cut our thumbs and pressed them together in a blood pact, believing that together we were going to be invincible."

"One term later and there was no Lindsey when I got to school. Oh no, here we go again, I thought. Hoping against hope that she was just poorly, I went to her aunt's house after school, to be told that her father had fetched her on the Saturday to live with him, as he and her mother had parted and would be getting divorced. I didn't know whether this was going to improve her life, as it seemed to me that he was the cause of her mother's breakdown, but I could say and do nothing. I asked her Aunt Jenny to let me have Lindsey's address and she said she would send it to me. I asked her to send it to my Gran's address as I didn't want it to get read or binned by anyone."

"Years went by. I went to Bakewell and I gave up on hearing from Lindsey, although I thought about her on and off for several years. To get this letter was exciting, but also a bit scary. Would it contain good news?"

"It was her writing on the envelope, a good sign. Hands trembling, I opened it quickly and let out a sigh of relief when it revealed that she was living in Birmingham, in a bedsit, and was working as a telephonist for the General Post Office. She would, she said, love to hear my news, and would love it even more if I could meet up with her in Birmingham!"

"I showed Brendon the letter and he got out his map, found Kings Heath and said he would drive us there on a Saturday which I would sort out with Lindsey. We met up around two weeks later. I introduced her to Brendon and gave her the biggest hug. We shed a few happy tears and both said in stereo, 'you haven't changed a bit!' at which all three of us laughed, and we then exchanged our news."

"She showed me a photo of her boyfriend, telling me that he was four years older than her and they had been together for two and a half years, and were engaged, hoping to marry in the autumn. Obviously, I was delighted for them both and her situation matched mine apart from the age difference, which she had no problem with. The afternoon went by so quickly, poor Brendon just sat watching and listening as we shared experiences, with the occasional comment if he was asked, and then it was time to exchange phone numbers and addresses and return to Sheffield. I was very happy then and kept smiling to myself as I remembered all of Lindsey's lovely mannerisms."

"I badgered Brendon about seeing the Vicar and organising our wedding, and he informed me that we should tell his parents and my Gran before doing any planning. I said I would tell my grandparents on my next visit, which would be mid-September, and we would both go to tell his parents before the end of September. The wedding would be before the new tax year, which I thought was a strange and unromantic way to remember such a romantic occasion, but I just wanted it to be settled, a date in my diary."

"I went to Beeston and broke the news to Granny, who wasn't surprised - in fact more than a little relieved, as she thought we were probably living together, although I assured her that we were not. She wasn't daft though and wanted to know that a wedding ring was going to be on my finger sooner rather than later."

"She suggested that she and I should go to Nottingham and have a look at wedding dresses in Jessops, then on to tea in Lyons tea shop. Oh Matthew, the excitement of it all was almost too much."

"It should be every girl's best time, preparing for her wedding, Julie."

"We went into Nottingham on the train and walked down to Slab Square and into Jessops. After holding up several meringue style dresses against me, the assistant noted my hysterical but muted laughter and decided that madam would better suit something longer, less ornate and narrow due to my small frame, and cream or ivory rather than white to accentuate my pale complexion, as white was too dramatic. She probably guessed that I was no virgin, I thought, but I nodded my approval when she brought a very elegant full-length fitted ivory silk dress overlaid with ivory Nottingham lace, with a satin ribbon and bow at the base of the zip at the back. It had a princess neckline and three-quarter plain silk sleeves. I tried it on and it was a perfect fit except for the length. Granny looked as if she was about to burst into tears, her bottom lip was doing its best to not wobble, so I turned to ask the assistant how much the dress was."

"'39 pounds 15 shillings and sixpence for the dress, 5 shillings to have it shortened,' said the assistant.

'I can shorten it myself, thank you,' I replied, thinking to myself that forty pounds was almost six weeks' wages, and preparing to say 'no, thank you.' I looked across at Gran with, I hoped, a shake-of-the-head and 'I can't afford it' kind of expression. To my surprise and delight Gran said the assistant could wrap it up and she got out her purse and paid for it."

"When the assistant had gone to do the wrapping and boxing of the dress, I sat next to Gran, picked up her age-spotted hands, looked straight into her eyes and said, 'thank you Granny, you're the best. I couldn't have paid that much, but you have always been there and given me the very best, haven't you?'

'Well somebody needed to. You didn't have the best start in life, did you? Anyway, no more nonsense. I'm pleased to know that there'll be somebody giving you the best when I can't. That is priceless.'"

Matthew struggled to show no emotion, but his eyes were moist.

"So we had a celebratory tea and cake in Lyons and I couldn't resist opening the box at one corner, tearing the tissue and admiring the beautiful lace-covered silk again. Back home at Gran's I wasted no time putting on the dress and standing on the dining table while Granny pinned the hem up. Grandpa walked in and his face was a picture."

'Oh Julie, you look a sight for sore eyes. He's a lucky man is Brendon.'"

"I had to phone Brendon, then, and tell him the news. His reaction wasn't as delighted as I had hoped, but he hadn't seen the dress, nor would he until we were in church on our wedding day."

"The dress came back to Sheffield and was placed in its box, hem turned up and ready, in Brendon's spare room, with strict instructions that it was only to be opened by me."

Chapter 54

"The time passed smoothly towards the weekend, when we were due to visit Brendon's parents."

"In the office, I had been talking about nothing else but the wedding for a week, describing the dress and the details surrounding its purchase, and the buzz filtered through to the office manager, who came down to our office to give his congratulations."

"We asked everyone to keep it to themselves as we hadn't told Brendon's parents about the wedding yet, but were going to do so on Friday night."

"Mr Bailey asked me their address and said that as he drove to Sutton-in-Ashfield every day from work, he could give me a lift there. I said I'd let him know later in the week and discussed the offer with Brendon. He said it made sense, as otherwise he'd have to drive from Repton back to Sheffield to pick me up, then back south to Sutton-in-Ashfield. It would save an hour-and-a-half and we would both get to his parents before 6 o'clock, which was when they had their evening meal."

"So the answer was 'yes please, I would be glad of a lift.'"

"Friday came and I took my packed

overnight bag into work. At 5 o'clock Mr Bailey came to my office with his coat on, briefcase in hand and we both made our way to his car. It was a dark blue sports car; in those days a car was a car to me and I made no distinction between them, so I couldn't tell you the make of it. I know I sat very low in the seat, reclined somewhat more than I felt comfortable with, and when he turned the key in the ignition the engine purred with a slight growl, and sped through the traffic like a warm knife through butter."

"In no time we were out of the city, surrounded by the shadowy peaks of Derbyshire, still magnificent although it was dusk, and the car lights were on. It was warm in the car and I was half asleep, but I was jolted awake when the car pulled off the road. The lights were off and Mr Bailey was opening the driver's door. I asked what had happened, then gasped with horror as he turned, his penis erect and out of his trousers."

"In no time he was on top of me, pulling a hole in the crotch of my tights, pressing the recline switch of the seat to maximum and then fumbling in my pants with his left hand."

"'No, no, stop it! I don't want …' I pleaded.

'Oh yes you do, Julie. I've seen it in your eyes and the way you prick tease me at work, so shut up and let's do it.'

'No, get off, stop it! I love Brendon and I don't want you or anybody else! Help!'"

"I couldn't breathe now, his weight crushing me and he was nearly inside me. I could feel the warm wetness of his penis fighting to penetrate me and my head started to reel, black waves of darkness taking over until the last thing I heard was him saying there was nobody there to help me and that it was a long walk to Sutton-in-Ashfield. Then I passed out."

"When I opened my eyes he was back in the driver's seat, looking disgruntled but dressed and tidy, and if it weren't for my clothes being out of place and a huge hole in my tights, no one would have guessed what had just happened. Except that I was shaking, sobbing and unable to move."

"'Well that was disappointing, Miss Brady,' he said. 'Shall we pretend it didn't happen? Actually, it didn't happen - at least not the way I wanted it to. But you had me worried there, you stopped breathing.'"

"He rearranged the seat, looked away while - still sobbing - I made myself tidy, and started the engine."

"'It's true what they say about you, the girls in the other office,' I blurted out between sobs. 'I know you're knocking off your secretary, Denise, and I've seen the secret looks between you and Marie. How many more of them are you screwing?'"

"'That would be telling,' he laughed mirthlessly. 'But you're not going to tell anyone, are you? If you do, I will make sure Brenda gets to hear my version.'

"Oh my God – Brendon! What should I do? Tell him? Not tell him? The consequences of either were equally unbearable."

"Why oh why did I accept this lift, knowing that Bailey was a womaniser - a womaniser with the power to make or break people? Because I honestly believed that my love for Brendon and his love for me was pure and true and that nothing could come between us or break that circle of pure love."

"But it had. And it was my fault. I wanted to die. Right then, right there. I pleaded silently, 'Oh God, please let me die!'"

Chapter 55

"Julie, good to see you. You were too upset to say goodbye last week, but I hope you took my advice and did something with the children to distract you and help you forget."

"Yes, Matthew. Once again retelling the awful event helps to write a line under it."

"The rest of the journey continued in silence, punctuated by sobs as I realised the gravity of my situation. Should I tell Brendon and hope that he would come to terms with the betrayal of both Daniel and myself? Throw myself on his mercy and trust that we could move on from the mess it would make?"

"Should I keep quiet and hope that Daniel Bailey would not betray me? Was that likely? I guessed that if I did, I would spend the rest of my days waiting for the letter, phone call, meeting or other ways that Daniel could find to hold my life in ransom."

"Arriving at Mabel Avenue, I got out of the car as fast as I could, pulling my skirt down to cover the massive hole in my tights and trying to rearrange my face so that it didn't look as distraught as I felt."

"Brendon's mum opened the door before I had a chance to ring the doorbell, she had been looking out for me. When she said "Hello love, come in" it was all I could do to not fall into her arms and sob out the whole sorry tragedy that I had suffered, but I gave her a weak smile and said I felt a bit carsick, and would she mind if I went upstairs to lie down?" Scrutinising my face, she observed that I did look somewhat pasty."

"I was dozing fitfully when Brendon arrived half an hour later, and he came straight upstairs, concerned about my state of health. Again, I fought the urge to recount the horror of my journey. Something made me hold back. At the same time, I knew I couldn't keep this up for long, but I felt genuinely ravaged in mind and body and needed to sleep. Brendon said he would leave me to rest and my meal would be saved in case I felt like getting up later, for which I was grateful."

"The night passed in fits of shaking: I was probably in shock. Nightmares came and went, mostly of me trying to escape from buildings, vehicles and being pursued by animals, monsters and deformed creatures which my subconscious mind created. Several times I woke up groaning or trying to scream, my mouth and throat dry and aching, and I was again thankful that someone had put a glass of water by the bed."

"Morning came and with it the dread - less now than yesterday, but I still felt fearful of the secret I had in my head. I decided instantly that whatever came out would not be here in his Mum's house, but back at the flat in Sheffield."

"We listened to the Beatles' Rubber Soul LP which Brendon had bought yesterday, went for a walk and chatted to his mum and dad. Their neighbour came round with her little girl, and we played with her and her dolls and I was kept sufficiently busy to not allow my thoughts to backtrack."

"Brendon said I looked better than I had looked yesterday and everyone seemed to accept that it was riding in a sports car, low down and close to the road, which had made me feel unwell. We decided that we would defer telling his mum and dad about our wedding plans until after we had spoken to the vicar and arranged a date, which was both a disappointment and a relief to me."

"Back in Sheffield, we had a few hours to spare and were both feeling the lack of intimacy that parents' houses tend to offer, and it wasn't long before we stripped off and went to bed. Brendon was in fine form and was as eager to please as usual, but I was in some kind of emotional lockdown and having never before been anything less than totally enjoying the pleasure of sex, I was at a loss. Brendon apologised and said he couldn't hold back any longer, and ejaculated, while I burst into tears."

"It all came out then. The whole horrible truth about why I had felt ill, about Daniel the sex-driven rapist, about me who had no way of knowing this could happen, no escape from something I truly did not want."

"Brendon was quiet throughout, his face changing through disbelief, rage, abhorrence and finally grief.

"'Why didn't you tell me on Friday?" he asked.'

'Because I didn't know how!' I answered."

Matthew interrupted. "Oh Julie, I hope he was able to see how it wasn't your fault. You thought he would throw you out of the car to walk if you didn't comply."

"It was stupid to think he really could do that, Matthew. I know that now, but it was different then. I was terrified."

Matthew nodded. "Even back then, in the sixties, it was always difficult to prove that a girl had been unwilling to have sex with a man she wasn't in a relationship with. You could have reported him to the police Julie, but there would be no guarantee that he would be punished, or that you would be believed."

"I felt dirty and used. A small part of me hoped that we could work it out. But I was not convinced because he took it so badly."

"Brendon was obviously very shocked by

the whole thing, Julie. We're out of time now, but you can tell me next week how you worked it out."

Chapter 56

"I just wanted Brendon to hold me, to tell me that he loved me, that everything would be okay. I expected him to be angry and to curse Daniel, even to want to give him a thrashing for what he had done to me. I thought he might insist that I leave Nichols Richardson and get a new job."

"He did none of these, but said he needed to think, to clear his head, and when I asked him if he still loved me, he said nothing, jumped out of bed, put on his clothes, then his coat and left the flat."

"I could feel panic closing in on me and realised that I was howling like a dog in pain. When I had exhausted myself, I got out of bed, dressed and went back to Tyzack Road, hoping that Daisy had gone to bed. She hadn't, but when she saw my face, she said I looked awful, and asked what the matter was. I said Brendon and I had had a falling out, and she nodded as if she was expecting to hear it."

"She made a cup of cocoa for us and tried to make me feel better, saying whatever it was would pass and we would be all right."

"We weren't all right though. I didn't want to go to work next morning and had been dreaming about confronting Daniel, waking often, glad that it was a dream, then realising that what he did to me was not a dream and I would have to face the reality of being in the same building as him, not knowing how he would behave and how he would treat me."

"Agonising about this made me late for work, which added to the stress factor. It was pouring with rain too, so I looked like a drowned rat when I finally reached my office. I got on with my work, head down and glancing frequently at the door, dreading the boss coming in, but I needn't have worried, he was as reluctant to face me as I was to face him."

"After a couple of days of being uncharacteristically quiet and withdrawn, Margaret sent Sandra out of the office to take the franking machine to the post office for a refill and asked me what was going on. I was flustered and pretended there was nothing, but she was an intuitive lady and had put two and two together and made four."

"'What's going on with you and Daniel Bailey?' she asked. I remained silent, looking at my feet.

'Has he been trying it on with you?'

I was shocked. 'Don't say anything!' I whispered. 'How did you know?'

'You're not the first and you won't be the last!' she replied. 'He hasn't been near this office since last Friday and that in itself says it all. He's not kept away since you started work here.'

"Was that true? Had I not noticed? No. I was so besotted with Brendon that I didn't even think about other men. I told Margaret that I had had to fight him off when he stopped the car and she showed no surprise whatever. She recounted the girls that had been in the same situation, most of whom had left, but there were a couple who were still working under his spell. Even her daughter had been one of Daniel's victims."

"Her face crumpled when she said this, and she went on to tell me that her daughter had had an abortion which Daniel had paid for."

"I was horrified. I didn't know what to say, what to do, what to think. Margaret composed herself and then asked what was I going to do."

"There was only one thing *to* do. I would start looking for another job."

Chapter 57

"It was close to Christmas, and I was spending less and less time at Brendon's flat."

"Brendon had changed. He was distracted, taking refuge in paperwork and other college business, and had put me off coming to the flat on several occasions saying he was going to be busy."

"We were not the couple we had been. I didn't feel that I was irresistible to him anymore, and when I asked him what was wrong, he said things were different but wouldn't enlarge on how or why. I just wanted him back."

"The week before we were due to see the vicar I went to the flat after work before Brendon got home. I sat at the table with a cup of tea, looking out across Sheffield. There was a pile of papers on the table and I idly shuffled through them, glancing at things and putting them back as I'd found them, until I came across a letter in an unfamiliar hand. My heart was doing backflips as I read."

'My dearest darling Brendon,

I can't stop thinking about you. Last Friday was unbelievable, we are so made for each other.

See you tomorrow!

ALL MY LOVE,

Sally
xxxxxxxxxxxxxxx'

Chapter 58

"It must have been a shock to see that letter, Julie?"

"You're not wrong Matthew. I was devastated. I went from disbelief to doubt, then from suspicion to certainty that it was from someone Brendon had met and had fallen in love with."

"When had it happened? Who was Sally? What did she mean about 'last Friday'? Ah yes, Brendon had said he was going to see his parents on Friday and wouldn't be back till today. Who the hell was she, then? How could Brendon do this? To ME?"

"Of course, I felt it was my fault. It was wrong to get in Daniel's car, wrong to believe that all he wanted to give me was a lift. Stupid girl! And after all, it was only to be expected. Somebody like me, unwanted, unloved, a maladjusted child, a worthless piece of rubbish, used and abused by those supposed to care for me. No wonder Brendon was looking for someone better…"

"Stop that now, Julie. He's not worth your tears. Do you hear me, it was *not your fault!* Brendon also used and abused you, and he was old enough and intelligent enough to know what he was doing. He would have lost his job and gone to prison if you had told the authorities what he did."

"But I loved him, Matthew and I believed that he loved me. He *did* love me. It was only after the Daniel incident that he stopped loving me."

"But Julie, if he had really loved you, he would have seen how traumatised you were by Daniel's disgusting behaviour and he'd have given you sympathy and understanding, would have stood by you and got over his own feelings. I would say that you were his 'trophy' which he no longer wanted as it had become tarnished. *NOT* your fault, Julie, you didn't deserve to be treated in that way. Brendon didn't deserve you."

"Well, he didn't want me, that much was obvious. How was I going to deal with it? The letter - had he left it for me to find? I wasn't in the habit of going through his paperwork, and he shared any letters with me that concerned me. I could pretend I hadn't seen it. But I *had* seen it and I was wounded, badly hurting and I had to get away, to decide what to do."

"All I really wanted was to die and not have to face what was inevitable. He didn't love me, somebody else loved him, I was going to lose him."

"I walked up and down Woodseats thinking and trying to plan my next move."

"I wanted to talk to Granny about it and get some advice, but couldn't face the thought of her knowing that it was all over for me. No wedding. No happy ever after. I went into the library and picked a book off the shelf, then sat at a table supposedly reading it. When a lady came over and asked if I was alright, I realised that silent tears were sliding down my face and the book was upside down. It was almost dark and the library was closing. I was no further forward with any ideas about what I should do."

"I walked across the road and turned up Cobnar Road to the point where I could see Brendon's flat. The light was on. I wanted to turn round and go back to Tyzack Road, but I also wanted to know if it was true that Brendon had got another lover."

"Running up the street and up the steps to the flat, I decided that I wouldn't use my key but would ring the doorbell. I don't know why I did that. Brendon answered the door and I could see straight away that he knew that I knew that he was done with me, and a strange look came over his face - partly guilt, partly fear and just a hint of denial."

"He said I had better come in and he would make a cup of tea. I said I didn't want a cup of tea, I wanted to know who Sally was."

"Sally was one of his students, he said. She

had been friendly with him for some time. How long? A couple of terms, but he wasn't 'seeing her' while we were together. Was he 'seeing her' now? Was he finishing with me now? Did he love her?"

"Long silence. I turned to go - I had my answer. He grabbed my hand as I turned and headed for the stairs and told me that things could never be the same since ... after ... 'you know.'"

"'Since Daniel attempted to rape me, you mean?'

"Of course! I was dirty now, soiled, vilified, tainted, impure. A filthy little tart waiting for the next man to seduce. I stormed out, yelling that he was a fine one to talk, calling him all the worst names I could think of."

"When I calmed down, I wondered what would have happened if I had told him about what the doctor had done to me as a child. Then I wondered if I could have kept it to myself forever and what might have happened if I couldn't. Either way, he would probably have replaced me with a younger version of someone who would worship him the way I did."

Matthew nodded sympathetically. "I'm afraid you're most certainly right about that. A paedophile will always be on the lookout for a younger victim, a virgin."

"I never saw him as a paedophile, Matthew. And I never will."

"After a couple of days feeling like the world was ending, I went up to Brendon's flat when I knew he wouldn't be there. I packed all my belongings into a suitcase - all except my wedding dress. This I laid out on the lounge floor then took out my dressmaking shears and cut it diagonally into five pieces. Then I walked out for the last time."

"I found a bedsitter in Hunters Bar, renting it for six months, got a second job as a barmaid at the The Black Swan, known fondly as the Mucky Duck, and wrote a long letter to Harriett telling her everything that had happened. She wrote back saying she was sorry that things hadn't worked out and could she come and stay over as we could have a night on the town? Naturally I was excited at the prospect of a night out with my best friend, and it cheered me up."

"Harriet arrived on the bus. We had a great night out and she told me that her family wanted me to spend Christmas with them. That was the best thing I could have wished for – something to look forward to."

"She also said that she was thinking of going to Germany as an au pair. German had never been for me, but I'd been top of the class in French and I quite fancied the idea of escaping to Paris as an au pair. It would seem strange if we were both in another country this time next year."

"Yes," Matthew said, "you'd both be in a place where you knew nobody else."

"Yes, and nobody would know ME. It would be easier to forget all the bad stuff."

"Harriet went home the next morning and I went to work. No sign of Daniel. It all began to seem dead to me, although I had enjoyed working when I'd had Brendon to go home to. I tried not to think about him, but it was impossible. If I hadn't had my job at the pub, I think I would have thrown myself in the River Sheaf."

"Even that job wasn't without problems, though. One of the barmen was getting rather too friendly and I almost gave up the job, then changed my mind and had a fling with him on a staff night out instead. I was disgusted with myself. I suppose I was proving that I wasn't unwanted. There was nothing other than lust on my part but he wanted more and it got awkward."

Chapter 59

"So, I kept myself busy and tried not to think about my future, empty as it would be. I tried to be angry with Brendon, but I felt as empty as my future looked. I punished myself by getting a razor comb and cutting off my hair and I starved myself as a penance for my sins."

"The other girls stared in disbelief when I showed up at work looking like a badly shorn sheep and quickly changed the subject, but I felt their pity. Margaret was concerned about me, but out of loyalty, never said anything other than to warn the girls to leave me alone. She arranged for a friend who was a hairdresser to come to my bedsit and do some damage limitation on my hair. I cried when I saw what a good job she had made of it, even though I hated my hair short."

"I wanted to look as dreadful as I felt, to justify being rejected."

"Eating had gone out of the window along with Brendon's love. I ate only when my body threatened to give up, and my clothes began to hang off me. I was weighed when I went to the doctor's surgery for pills to help me sleep at night and was seven stone four pounds, about a stone less than usual. My periods had stopped. I stopped taking my contraceptive pills and started drinking cheap wine. This got me through

December and suddenly it was nearly Christmas."

"I'd told my Granny that Brendon and I were having some time apart and she didn't mind when I said I was spending Christmas with Harriet in Grindleford. No doubt she wondered what was going on, but she didn't push it, and I said I would come over on December 27th and stay a few days."

"Christmas Eve duly arrived and we waited for the word to come round that we could leave work at 3 pm and not come back till 2nd January - and I was surprised when Daniel came into our office to deliver the news personally. He walked past my desk, said Merry Christmas to us all, turned round and walked out again. No recognition of my presence whatsoever."

"I was relieved for a moment, then furious. I was nothing to him, yet he had caused me to lose everything that was good in my life. He didn't care a fig about any girl who crossed his path, and I *was* any girl."

"I had brought my suitcase to work and I lugged it to the bus station to catch the bus for Grindleford. The journey stopped my feelings from sinking any lower. Derbyshire is beautiful at any time, but watching the sun set over the hills lifted my mood and the idea of spending Christmas in a busy, happy family atmosphere bucked me up. So much so that when I walked up the lane to Harriet's house, I arrived with a big smile on my face."

"We exchanged news and when a cup of tea was offered, Harriet said she and I would go to the pub and catch up instead, and her elder brother said he would join us, if that was okay. A couple of hours later we rolled back to the cottage quite merry and were treated to a waft of the delicious aroma of Christmas dinner, which proved to be as good as it promised. As there were so many of them, Harriet's family always had Christmas dinner on Christmas Eve and Christmas Day usually a buffet-style meal, with people coming and going, neighbours dropping in for a glass of sherry and a mince pie, friends, girlfriends, boyfriends etc turning up and welcomed."

"I really felt part of the family, and safe and warm amongst them even though my heart was breaking and my life falling apart. Then a frisson of guilt wiped the smile from my face. I was here under false pretences. I was nothing like them - had lied and lied again to gain entry into their family. I had to do something about it, even if it meant being thrown out, shunned, despised, whatever might result from the disclosure."

"'I have something to tell you all,' I said, looking down at my plate. I could feel the atmosphere freeze momentarily."

"'Well go on, then,' Harriet said, looking curious. 'Don't keep us in suspense!'

'I don't have five brothers!' I muttered. 'I only have two!'

"Silence fell and they all looked at each other. Suddenly Harriet's Mum put her hand to her mouth and tittered. Then they all began laughing and in less than a minute we were all wiping our eyes and nearly falling off our chairs in mirth."

"I was forgiven, and told it was the best kept secret they had ever been honoured to have revealed to them; it had absolutely made their day. I loved them all, and spent two happy days with them."

"Harriet's elder brother James showed some interest in me, which boosted my ego. Although I liked him and thought he would make a good partner, I felt no chemistry between us; and when he started talking about the future - marriage, children, all the things I had visualised with Brendon - I found myself shuddering at the thought of sharing them with anyone else."

"This, and the lack of physical attraction to any man, was to stay with me for a long time. If you'd asked me then how I saw my future, my hopes for a happy life with a perfect man, I would have said that was a blank page, one of many."

"Later, Harriet showed me the nannying job in the Lady Magazine she was applying for in Germany. I looked at the ones offering au pair positions in France and let Harriet talk me into applying for a job in Paris, feeling fairly certain that I'd hear nothing back. We spent a day reminiscing about school, boys and men, and the difference between them, and I soaked up as much of family life as I could."

"You needed to do that, Julie. Again, you were fortunate in having Harriet as a friend along with her family. Next week, then?"

Chapter 60

"It was time to go to Beeston and tell Granny the whole sad story, and I didn't look forward to it at all."

"Harriet waved me off with her usual cheeky grin and a blown kiss, and I almost got off the bus at the next stop to go back and beg her family to adopt me. But I knew that would just add to the list of injuries to report to Grandma."

"When I got to Beeston, I tapped on the back door, opened it and there was Granny. Her face told me immediately that she knew something. But how could that be? I hadn't told anyone who was in touch with her."

"She stepped towards me and opened her arms. In an instant, the flood gates opened and I was sobbing out my pain on her shoulder, held tightly by her arms and her love. I cried my heart out until my face ached."

"Granny said we would have a cup of tea and an egg custard from Birds, which was only bought as a real treat or for lessening pain. They were quite difficult to get right cooked in her aga, too, so one of the very few shop-bought cakes and puddings on offer in her home. I asked how she knew that Brendon and I had separated and she paused, looked out of the window, back to me and told me that he had phoned her. I sat upright in disbelief."

"'Brendon phoned you? When? Why? What did he say?'

'He said that he was very sorry to tell me that your relationship had ended.'

'Did he say why?'

'He said he had met someone else.'

'Was that all he said?'

'No, he said that he hadn't had a chance to explain it all as you wouldn't give him the opportunity.'

'What's to explain, Granny? He loved me, he met her, now he doesn't love me anymore because he loves *her*. Simple.'

'In my experience, matters of the heart are never simple. Your grandpa never once told me he loved me until he became very ill and I thought I was going to lose him.'

'When was that?'

'When your Dad was 11 years old. We had been married for 15 years!'

'Well anyway, I don't understand why he rang you. I suppose it's because he hadn't got the guts to explain it to me himself.'

'It took some courage to telephone me, Julie, think about it. He didn't know how I would react. And he had to talk to me to get to you …'

And she told me that Brendon had arranged

to come and see me. 'He's going to take you somewhere where he can do the decent thing and finish things properly.'"

"Well, Matthew, that started me off again. How dare he! As if it wasn't enough to trash my feelings by leaving that letter for me to find, now he wanted to drag them through the mud again with a biopsy of what went wrong and why. *He* gets to end up happy and with a new life, a new love and *I* just want to die. I cried, yelled, stamped my feet and swore I would kill him. And Granny just let me get on with it: she understood why I might feel that way, just as she understood most things about me."

"I have to admit that I couldn't bring myself to tell her about the wedding dress, but then she never asked. Instead, she said I was too thin and we would do something about that."

"So, Julie, did Brendon come and take you out to explain everything?"

"Oh yes, Matthew, he came. He tried to stick a smile on his face, which slid off when I gave him the most disdainful look I could muster – down and up and down again."

"He greeted my Gran and I could feel her shooing us out without us needing to turn around. We got in his car and he drove to Attenborough gravel pits, which is now a nature reserve. He parked up and waited, neither of us wanting to initiate the conversation, both observing the water and the birds through opposite windows."

"Finally, he said he was sorry. I replied that I was sorry, too - sorry I had ever trusted him. He looked at me and put his hand over mine, telling me that that hurt. Even then, just the touch of his hand on mine made me long to hold him, kiss him, beg for a chance to forget all that had led up to this moment. To start again."

"Desperate and hopeful, I said it wasn't too late to turn back the clock. Foolish, stupid, naïve girl - his face told me before he spoke the words that it wasn't going to happen. He loved Sally, he said, and was going to marry her next June."

"I pulled the engagement ring off my finger and flung it at him, screaming that he'd better give it to Sally. He retrieved it and put it back in my hand while I was yelling and crying and wanting to run away. I wound down the car window and threw the ring as far as I could, then said he had better take me back to Beeston."

"Brendon wasn't going to leave the ring in the undergrowth, and he didn't want to drive his manic screaming ex-girlfriend anywhere, so he got out of the car and set to looking for it. That took almost half an hour, by which time I had almost regained control of myself. He drove me back and I got out of the car, slammed the door and ran up the drive without saying a word or looking back."

"Granny had heard the car door slam and was in the kitchen waiting for me. She put a finger to her lips and said quietly that I should get ready for bed, that she would bring me a cup of tea and we could talk everything over."

"She reappeared with a cup of tea for each of us and said she had taken Gramps a cup and told him I was feeling under the weather. She would explain everything to him when the time was right. She knew I was suffering, and there was nothing she could say or do to make it right, but I owed it to myself to get over the heartbreak and make a new life for myself. It wasn't going to be easy, she said, especially as Brendon had seemed to be 'the one', but most women had to kiss a lot of frogs before they found Prince Charming."

"That did make me smile, but I vowed that I had no wish to kiss any man for a very very long time. Granny stayed for an hour, refilled my cup of tea and left me listening to my radio after she'd assured me that not only would I survive this episode of my life, but I would find a way of making changes and improving my status, whatever that meant."

"How ever did she get to be so wise Matthew?"

"By learning from experience, I expect, and having empathy and a willingness to help others in need. You were very fortunate in having her, Julie. She obviously loved you very much."

"Yes, she did. I suppose she was one of the angels I was promised."

"Angels? What do you mean?"

"Do you remember me saying I had a mountain top experience on holiday in the Lake District, literally at the top of a mountain, where I heard a voice saying angels would look after me? Silly, really - if there *is* a God, why would He want to help me? I mean, look how rubbish my life has been so far."

"I can't comment on the subject of God and angels, Julie but you are here, you are doing okay, and you have a lot going for you, with lots of good things to remember. But tell me, what happened next?"

"I went back to Sheffield. Waiting for me on the doormat was a letter from Harriet telling me she'd got the job in Germany and was going there in mid-January. She hoped I would be as successful."

"And two days later, the letter arrived to say that I was! Soon, I too would be leaving – leaving England, leaving my broken heart with the man that I loved, and leaving the employ of the company that also employed the man who had forcibly broken my dreams."

Chapter 61

"So what did you do then, Julie?"

"I set about getting a passport, references, everything necessary to leave England. Getting a photograph for my new passport, getting details from the agency about the family I would be living with and sorting out the bedsit gave me enough to think about. I had all my train times and ferry crossing details written down, checked and verified."

"I packed my school trunk, which Brendon had arranged to be delivered to my bedsit, to send in advance by rail, and somehow got through the weeks till March in a kind of mental fog."

"My leaving do from Nichols Richardson was Friday lunchtime in the Fat Cat pub on Alma Street. My workmates had bought me a pair of frilly knickers (for when I got a job at the Moulin Rouge) and a travel alarm clock which was useful and much smaller than the big, noisy metal clock I used at home. It was a special time and made me realise that I would miss my co-workers, especially Margaret, and we shed a few tears together as I closed the door on my old life. Daniel hadn't come into work that day so I was spared having to spend time with him. Good riddance, I decided."

"As my friends went back to work I went back to the bedsit for the last time and checked that everything was in order for my departure to another life in France."

"I had to leave the flat in Hunters Barr so I put all my stuff in my old school trunk and took it to Granny's on the train."

"I couldn't face going to say goodbye to Dad, so I told him over the phone. He said he would miss me and wished me the best."

"And what about your mother, Julie? Did you go and say goodbye to her?"

"No need - by that time she'd buggered off to Wales."

"What on earth made her move to Wales?"

"There was a new man on the scene apparently, but I'm not sure anybody really believed that."

"So, the day arrived and found me on the train to St Pancras, too excited to read my book, too nervous to think beyond the next train. I went over the things I could say in French, acting out scenarios in my head and finding that my vocabulary wasn't up to dealing with the numerous situations I might encounter. On the train from St Pancras to Dover I did manage a few chapters of 'The Magus' by John Fowles, and closed my eyes for a while. In my carrier bag were snacks and cold drinks, which I was glad to eat and drink."

"Why was that, Julie? Were you too scared to go to the dining car?'"

"Yes, Matthew. Brendon had always done that sort of thing before and now I was having to travel alone. Granny had made me some sandwiches, scones and apple turnovers and put crisps and a bottle of Corona in a cake tin. I should, she said, beware of eating and drinking anything from the buffet on the train as you didn't know how long it had sat there! She'd held me close and told me to be good, and if I couldn't be good, I was to be careful - making me smile and preventing the inevitable tears. I smiled to myself at the memory and then I could hear the gulls and taste the ozone in the air as we arrived at the ferry port."

"It was easy enough to board the ferry as a foot passenger. I found a seat, took off my coat and laid it on an empty seat along with my carrier bag, asking the lady in the next seat to keep an eye on everything for me."

"Then I headed up to the deck. I gave up trying to keep my chin-length hair from blowing in my face and I gripped the handrail at the rear of the boat, staring as the ferry left its wake. I fought the urge to take Brendon's ring off my finger and drop it into the sea, along with my broken heart, broken dreams and the memories of the men who had broken them."

"The White Cliffs became smaller and smaller as I watched them and I had a moment of sudden panic at the thought of leaving everything familiar. I was going to a place far from everything and everyone I knew, a place where I would be truly alone. This was not Sheffield, where I could hop on a train and go back and seek help and comfort from my Gran."

"Then I felt a dizzying feeling of euphoria as the adrenalin rushed in, making my heart pound with a sense of the adventure that was awaiting me. I found myself smiling."

"Au revoir England,' I said to myself.

Jean Taylor

Jean Taylor was born in Nottingham during the post-war baby boom and lived in the region – sometimes with family, sometimes under local authority care – until early adulthood gave her the freedom to leave the area and travel.

Since then, Jean has lived in various areas of the Midlands and South Yorkshire, as well as - for a short time - overseas. After retirement from the National Health Service, Jean moved to Leicestershire, where she now lives with her husband David, sharing between them four children and three grandchildren.

'Maladjusted' is Jean's first book.

Printed in Great Britain
by Amazon